Touching Gloves

The life of a female champion fighter

Serena Ward aka Viper Girl

A lesbian story based in the sport of boxing

A story by Shiralyn J. Lee, author of LGBT novels and shorts.

Touching Gloves

ISBN-13: 978-1502751362
ISBN-10: 1502751364

Copyright

Contents

Touching Gloves

INTRODUCTION

Serena Ward is an undefeated champion boxer. This story focuses on her personal background and commences with her girlfriend Holly showing signs of unrest in their relationship as it is at the point of breaking.

Her erratic sister Dawn, finds out that her husband is cheating on her and resorts to doing her own detective work to catch him at it.

Serena's passion for fighting in the ring is tested when she is challenged to an ultimate fight.

CHAPTER ONE

With her left eye closed, swollen and split across the brow, Serena Ward, or as she is publicly known as, 'Viper Girl,' walked out of the ring, with another win behind her, continuing her reign as the undefeated champion. At her side, Ricky Koch, her manager, cheered loudly. He, along with Serena, paraded through the cheerful crowd, their arms were raised and their fists punching the air.

"Serena, I love you," a female fan holding her hand over her heart, shouted over the loud roaring mass.

"Over here, Serena," a photographer called to her.

Serena turned and posed triumphantly in front of the camera, showing off her muscular body that glowed with sweat. With her emotions running high, she grabbed hold of Ricky and pulled him next to her to pose with him. Relishing in the victory, he pulled her hair tie from her ponytail and ruffled her hair to give her a sexier appearance. She looked directly at the camera and roared fiercely.

"Serena, do you think that there will ever be an opponent who can beat you?" a reporter shouted to her.

"If she's out there and she thinks she stands a chance, then bring it on baby!" she screamed back.

Fans were holding their hands out in hopes of Serena high-fiving them as she walked past. A few were lucky enough to be granted their wish.

"Serena, we need to get you to the locker room," Ricky informed her. He rested his arm over her muscular shoulder and swayed her toward the exit.

In the locker room, Serena sat on a bench. She unwrapped the soft gauze from her hands and spread her fingers out, stretching them slowly.

Ricky stood behind her, massaging her shoulders and giving her the low down on her opponent. "You are undefeatable. Shit! If I was a lesbian, I'd kiss you!" he said, handing her a bottle of water. "Here, drink this, you need it. Now let's get the doctor to see to that eye."

A few minutes later the cut doctor walked into the locker room and examined Serena's eye. He stuck medical tape across her brow and instructed her to use an ice pack over the swelling.

"Is Holly here?" Serena asked Ricky, peering behind him in hopes of her girlfriend walking in to surprise her.

Ricky looked down at his watch and then at Serena. "She didn't turn up, at least, I didn't see her and her seat was empty throughout the match."

"Where's my phone, I need to call her," Serena said, getting up to search through her locker for her phone. Finding it, she called Holly's number. It went straight to voicemail. "For fuck sake, where the hell is she?"

Ricky shrugged his shoulders. "How the fuck should I know?" he replied.

Serena picked up the bottle of water and unscrewed the top. Gulping it down quickly, she paced the room, frustrated at her girlfriend's lack of support. Her anger had gotten the better of her, causing her to slap the wall to at least satisfy her antagonism. "What the hell is wrong with her now?"

Before Ricky could give his opinion, he heard his name being called out in the hallway and peered out to acknowledge that it was time for Serena's interview. "Come on, Viper Girl, it's time to put your smile back on for the cameras," he told her.

Reporters and camera men were waiting in the interview room. Adora, Viper Girl's defeated opponent, had walked in first and sat herself down.

"Adora, can you tell us what's going through your mind, right now?" a reporter asked.

"Apart from feeling disappointed at myself, you mean?" she replied with a contempt attitude.

Viper Girl, holding an ice pack over her eye, walked in with her manager. They sat down next to Adora and her manager, acknowledging them both with a nod.

The reporters then freely fired their questions.

"Viper Girl, do you think that your undefeated record is due to the professional relationship that you have with Ricky?"

"Of course I do, well, partly anyway, I have Pete to thank for my training. Ricky is a great manager, yeah, he's strict when he needs to be and that's what I love about him but he's also a big softie too, aren't you," she laughed, looking at him.

"What she said," he replied and smiled at the reporters with his two thumbs up.

"Adora, do you think that there was anything you could have done to change the outcome of the fight?"

Adora rolled her eyes defiantly. "Anyone can look back in hindsight. I mean really, what kind of question is that?" she responded with her arms crossed over her chest.

"Viper Girl, how are things on the home front? We noticed the absence of Pink Leopard tonight. Is everything okay with you two and what's she going to say about your eye?"

A few muted giggles were heard amongst the crowd.

"Let's keep it to professional questions and not personal ones, hey boys," Ricky advised them.

"It's all good," Viper Girl yelled out. "And yeah, I'll be keeping this ice pack on for a while, doctors' orders."

"Adora, you were knocked out, do you feel cheated at all?"

"No, I don't." She turned to her manager and whispered in his ear that she'd had enough.

"I think we'll cut it there, gentlemen, thank you for your patience," her manager said, getting up out of his seat. He shook Viper Girls hand, then Ricky's hand and walked out with Adora, who completely blanked her opponent.

"Congratulations, Viper Girl," some of the reporters commented.

"Thanks guys," Ricky said. He got up and encouraged Viper Girl to do the same. They left the room and headed back to the locker room.

Serena showered, then dressed in a black V-neck t-shirt and jeans.

"I already know what the answer is but do you want to go for a celebratory drink?" Ricky asked her.

"You know I can't, Ricky. I have to go home and find out why Holly didn't show tonight. I know we've been going through some shit lately but she could have at least called or text me to let me know she wasn't coming."

Ricky picked up his jacket that had been hanging on the back of a chair and plucked his car keys from the inside pocket. He jiggled them in his hand. "Okay, come on, I'll drive you home."

They got into his yellow Porsche and drove off down the street.

Serena tried to call Holly again but she still doesn't answer. "For Christ sake, why the hell isn't she answering her phone? Is she completely stupid?"

Ricky glanced at her, then back to the road. "Trouble in paradise?"

"No!" Serena lifted her butt up slightly and shoved her phone into her front pocket. "I see you've tidied the car up, what's the occasion?" she said, snooping in the glove box.

"Ah you don't miss a thing, do you?" he replied smiling, and happily tapped his hands on the steering wheel.

They pulled up on to the driveway in front of her two storey house and were greeted by a neighbor who was walking her white Maltese dog. She approached the car and tapped on the passenger window. Serena pressed the button to open it.

The woman bent down to speak to Serena. "I saw you, on the TV, you won the fight, congratulations." Before she could carry on saying anything else, her dog barked at a passing car, much to Serena's annoyance.

"Yeah, thanks, Rhonda."

"Okay, well I'll be off now. Just wanted to say, well done." She walked away, tugging on the leash to make her dog follow.

Serena got out of the car and walked around to Ricky's side and leaned in to his open window. "Go and have a drink for me, okay."

"Maybe I'll have a few for you. Now go and get some well-deserved rest and keep that energy for the ring, I know you and Holly can work things out. But it still amazes me how you rule in your profession and yet can't keep tabs on the lady at home. Okay, say hi to Holly for me." He reversed the car back into the street and drove off. Sounding his car horn, he waved out of the window.

Serena opened her front door and called out for Holly. There was no answer. Instead, her partially blind cat, Sprott, came running down the hallway toward her, meowing and then working a figure eight around her ankles. She picked him up and held him to her chest. His long whiskers tickled her face as he nudged her lovingly.

"Hey, Sprott, and what have you been up to? Have you been left all alone?" she said to him adoringly and stoked his head. She carried him into the kitchen and placed him down on the gray slate floor. "Sprott, want some dinner, hey?" she asked him. She opened the cupboard above the refrigerator and took a can of meat out. Sprott meowed loudly. His black bushy tail stood to attention and quivered with excitement as he watched her fix his meal. She opened the can and as she emptied the contents into his bowl, he stretched his front legs up the base cupboard door and scratched his claws into the mahogany wood. "Sprott! No!" She shunted him away with her foot, then placed his bowl down on his feeding mat. "There you go."

She tickled his head and then went to the fridge to grab a beer. Typically, Holly had stacked food items in front and shoved the beers to the back of the fridge shelf. Serena reached in, moving a bag of peaches and a watermelon out of the way, she grasped a bottle. Tossing the cap into the garbage, she then made her way through the house to find out where Holly could possibly be. She swigged her beer and then called out Holly's name. Holly didn't answer. She walked through the lounge and opened the patio door to see if Holly was lounging by the pool. Her suspicion was correct. Holly was relaxed on a sun lounger. She had tall glass of orange juice and vodka on the table to the side of her and, was what seemed like to Serena, soaking up the sun in her bold orange bikini.

Serena, irritated, walked up to her. "What the fuck, Holly? You've been here all this time? I tried calling you, damn it, Holly, and damn you!" She swigged her beer back hard and stood in front of Holly with her mouth pursed and her hands on her hips.

Holly removed her sunglasses and slapped them down next to her drink. She pushed herself up and sat on the side of the lounger. "I got my fucking period!" she snarled. She stood up and with a look of disdain, she stormed off inside the house.

Serena stared blankly at the patio door for a moment, allowing time for Holly's information to absorb. "Shit! Shit! Fucking shit!" She immediately ran into the house, through the lounge and out to the hallway. "Holly!" she shouted.

Holly had almost reached the top of the stairs and hearing her name, she stopped and held on to the banister.

Half-turning her head, she wiped a tear streaming from her eye. "I'm never going to conceive, am I?" She took another step to the top stair, walked along the balcony and disappeared into the bedroom where she threw herself down onto their king-size bed and screamed into her pillow.

Serena traipsed up the stairs and stopped at the bedroom doorway. She leant into the door frame with her hand rested high against it. "Baby, I'm sorry, maybe we can try again soon—."

Holly lifted her head up from the pillow to look at Serena. "Again? Do you honestly think that I can keep doing this to myself? Look at me, look at what this has done to me! I hate myself, I hate this, I hate everything, I hate you and I even hate Sprott." She threw herself back down into the pillow where her screams were once again muffled.

Serena entered the room and sat on the edge of the bed. She stroked Holly's back to comfort her. "Whatever you want, babe, whatever you want." Her sadness revealed itself through her softened voice.

Holly, realizing that Serena was hurting as much as she was, stopped crying and turned over to face her. "Oh my god, your eye." She sat up and viewed Serena's injury closer. "Does it hurt?" she asked her softly.

"Nah, I'm fine. I'm more concerned about you and about us, and really, you hate Sprott?"

"I know, it was a stupid thing to say. I was just hoping that we would be pregnant by now and every month it's the same thing, no baby!"

Serena gently kissed Holly's forehead. "We'll get through this, I promise." She took hold of Holly's hand and brushed the back of it against her cheek. "Hey, I won again and apparently, you were missed today. "

"Oh no, were they asking for me or Pink Leopard?"

"What do you think?" Serena winked her eye playfully and smiled.

They laid down together on the bed, with Holly facing the window and Serena spooning her, they soon fall asleep.

The air was humid and throughout the night, a storm was building. In the early hours, a fork of lightning struck over the city, followed by a reverberating roll of thunder. Serena jolted from her sleep and sat up quickly to find that Holly was not next to her. A second rumble of thunder sounded over the house and when Serena looked to the window, she found Holly standing in front of it, staring at the sky that was being lit up with streaks and flashes of white light.

"Holly, what are you doing? Come away from there," Serena asked her.

"Isn't it beautiful? Just look at it. Just for a brief moment, the city looks alive in the dead of the night, every time the lightning strikes." She turned and looked at Serena. Her eyes were filled with emotional tears.

Serena got out of bed and stood at her side. She looked out of the open window and watched the electrical storm with her girlfriend. "Yes, it is beautiful." Hugging Holly from behind, and using her chin, she nudged Holly's hair away from her neck and planted a kiss. "We are all right, aren't we? she asked, unsure of how Holly's mind was thinking.

Serena's hands were clasped together at Holly's waist. Holly placed her hands over them and squeezed gently. She nodded her head faintly and Serena felt that she was acting a little distant toward her.

Another clap of thunder cracked over the house, immediately followed by a fork of lightning, striking closely. The two women, still in their embrace, shuffled backwards toward the bed until Serena felt the mattress pressed up against the backs of her legs. They climbed back into bed and listened to the storm above them.

Holly managed to fall asleep quickly but Serena had a mind full of chatter. She stared at the ceiling and continually self-questioned her relationship. She turned onto her side and gazed at Holly. She whispered the words, "Am I going to lose you?" Then she closed her eyes.

CHAPTER TWO

The morning air was warm and fresh and drifted into the bedroom through the open window. A blue cloudless sky had replaced the storm, in fact, everything seemed serene as a light breeze entered the room, causing the white chiffon drapes to shimmer.

Sprott came trundling into the bedroom meowing noisily for his breakfast. He jumped up onto the bed and began to massage the gray floral duvet cover.

Serena stirred and reached out to pat him. "Sprott, please let me sleep a bit longer," she murmured.

He tramped up toward her face and began to nudge her shoulder, purring and licking her arm in the process.

Holly opened her eyes and with a sleepy voice, asked, "Hun, what time is it?"

Serena looked at the clock on the bedside table. "It's 6.20am."

"Seriously? That's way too early. Sprott, get off the bed. Serena, don't encourage him. He's shedding black fur everywhere," Holly complained.

Serena threw back the duvet and got out of bed. "Come on, Sprott, I'll feed you." Still half asleep, she carried him downstairs to the kitchen and fed him. Whilst he ate, she leant over the sink, resting her hands on the edge of the countertop and looked out of the window. Rhonda was outside again, walking her dog and it looked as though she was having to discipline him for trying to chase after a neighbor's cat. "I'm so glad you're an indoor cat, Sprott," she said, looking down at him.

Holly made her presence known when she entered the kitchen a few minutes later. "Oh, is the coffee made yet?" She flicked her blond hair away from her face as she walked over to the countertop. Picking up the coffee pot and seeing that it was empty, she looked disappointed that Serena hadn't yet made it.

Serena sighed. "I'll make it now. So I take it that you've decided to give getting pregnant a miss."

"Yep. I'm done with being poked and prodded like I'm some sort of experiment. I recognize that it was me who pushed for us to have a baby but to be honest, I gave up my fighting career to do this. My body muscle has gone, I think my sanity has been tried and tested way too many times and well, yeah, I want my life back."

"Just like that, you'd throw it all away because it's taken longer than we thought it would."

"We, you're saying we as if it's been you're body and your career that's been messed up. How many times did you ever think to call me whilst you were away touring and just ask me, hey, are we pregnant today? Not once, Serena, not once!"

Serena opened the cupboard door up forcefully and grabbed the bag of coffee beans. She removed the top from the grinder and poured the beans in. "I was working, Holly. I've been trying to provide a secure future for us both. Do you honestly think that I like having an eye like this?"

"You can fix your eye, Serena, I can't fix not getting pregnant!"

Serena turned the grinder on. It was loud. "I can't hear you," she shouted over the noise.

"Oh just forget it, I'll buy one while I'm out." She left the house slamming the door hard behind her.

Serena watched her through the window as she opened her car door. Rhonda called 'Hello' to her from her front yard but Holly just waved her hand without even looking at her. She got into her car, reversed it into the street and sped off.

Sprott wandered over to Serena and brushed his head up against her leg, then meowed.

"At least you appreciate me, hey, Sprott." She said.

Serena spent most of the morning lounging by the side of the pool. Over the past few weeks, she had been in training for yesterday's fight and today was her first to relax. She lay on the wooden lounger, wearing her sunglasses and her toned body slathered in sun cream. She was trying to go through her emails and messages on her tablet but her mind kept wandering back to her feelings about Holly. She had been feeling insecure about their

14

relationship lately and with Holly's outburst that morning, gave her even more reason to believe her own doubts.

Her phone was next to her on the side table. She had set it to silent and not noticed that she had already missed two calls. On the third call, the phone vibrated against her glass of orange juice, which alerted her to it.

She picked it up and saw her sister's number on the screen. "Hi, Dawn, what's going on with you?" she asked casually.

'Hey, I'm on my way over to pick you up. Mom's been involved in an incident.'

Serena sat up quickly. "Is she all right, what happened?" she asked, already making her way inside the house to get dressed.

'I'm not sure yet. There was a message left on my phone by an Officer Hansen to come to the credit union. I'll be at yours in about two minutes, be ready.'

"Okay, I'm getting dressed now, bye." Serena ran up the stairs to her bedroom and grabbed the first item she saw in her wardrobe. She rapidly dressed in her yoga pants and vest top, slipped on her runners and ran back down stairs. She went through the house, locking the sliding patio door, checking that the windows were all shut and making sure that Sprott had plenty of kibble and water for the day. She picked up her hoodie top, wallet and phone and went to the front door, where Dawn was just pulling up into the front drive way.

Before Serena had even buckled up her seat belt, they were already driving down the street.

"Hey, slow down, Dawn, I'd like to get there alive," Serena told her sternly, still trying to click the metal tongue into the buckle.

"Okay, okay, I'm just worried about mom. I wish I'd have been able to speak to the Officer instead of receiving a short message. I mean, is it bad that mom didn't phone me herself? All I can think of, is that she's either tried to rob the bank or—"

"Or what, Dawn?" Serena asked.

"Or, what if there's been a robbery and mom was caught up in some sort of shooting and she's hurt and she's lying there, scared and dying and her last wish was to have her daughter's at her side before she dies? Oh god, Serena, my mind is filled with crazy thoughts."

"Now why would mom need to rob a bank? And if there had been a shooting or any kind of attempted robbery, wouldn't it be on the news by now? I think that your mind has gone into overkill."

Dawn slowed her speed when she realized that she was thinking way too irrationally. They approached a red traffic light and waited at the junction for it to change. Although Serena had made Dawn see sense, Dawn still couldn't help feeling edgy, and her nerves began to flare up again when the lights didn't change fast enough.

"I swear to god that I'm always on the road that takes the longest for the lights to change. Just look at how many cars are going through on the other side. I'm so fed up with lights, there's too many of them. How can they call these roads highways, when they have so many lights to stop the flow of traffic?" Dawn rambled on. She hit the horn three times in anger, thinking that that would make them change.

"Dawn, I love you, but you are really freaking me out with your behavior. Mom will be fine, okay." Serena placed her hand on Dawns leg and gently rubbed it.

Dawn, gripping the steering wheel so tight, that her knuckles were turning white, bowed her head down and smacked it, not too hard, into the steering wheel, then let out an almighty scream. "It's not mom, she's not the problem, well she is but she's not the reason why I'm so stressed out."

The lights changed for them to go. Because Dawn had her head buried into the steering wheel, she wasn't aware that they had changed. The driver in the car behind them, sounded his horn and ranted as he stuck his head out of the window and then continued to sound his horn. Dawn and Serena were oblivious to his behavior.

"What's wrong, Dawn, what's happening to you to cause you to react like this?" Serena asked softly, concerned that her sister was about to have a nervous breakdown.

Dawn, now in floods of tears, lifted her head and looked at Serena. "I don't want to hear, I told you so, not from

17

you, Serena. It's Phil, he's having an affair." She cried again, loudly.

The driver behind was infuriated and got out of his car. He walked up to Dawns window and banged on it angrily. Dawn looked up at him, her mascara was running down her face, her mouth wide and crooked from crying. She actually made for an ugly crier!

"You're the worst driver in the world," the man shouted to her through the glass.

Dawn, feeling even more intimidated by this complete stranger whom she had no idea that she had held up, cried even louder and harder. "Now even strangers are approaching me and telling me that I'm useless," she bawled, looking at her sister.

Serena got out of the car and walked around to the man. Her 5ft 9inch muscular physique was quite threatening to his 5ft 6inch slim build. Because her arms and shoulders were on show, she flexed her biceps, showing her mighty physical empowerment over this guy. She didn't have to say a word, he just backed away and got into his car.

Before he closed his door, he muttered, "The lights are about to change to green."

Serena nodded and got back inside her sisters car. She buckled up and then sympathetically told her sister that the lights had changed to green.

"See, I told you that I always get stuck with the longest red light," Dawn sobbed, trying to drive and blow her nose at the same time.

"Yes, Dawn, I think you're right," Serena agreed, just to humor her. "How do you know that Phil is having an affair? Has he told you about it, did you catch him out?"

"I needed to use his laptop this morning as mine lost the will to live last night. Well that was after I threw it across the room during an argument with him. God he can be so pathetic at times, don't you think, Serena? I mean, when we argue, we always have great make-up sex but last night, he was being a complete jerk."

"He always has been," Serena mumbled.

"What? Anyway, he wouldn't listen to me, he just kept yelling over my screams."

"Are you listening to yourself here?" Serena asked sarcastically.

"No way, Serena, no way am I in the wrong here. If I hadn't thrown my laptop at him in temper, I wouldn't have found out about 'stick thin Cynthia,' his secretary. I always felt that she had her beady eyes on him. And that chin, my god, it's like a witches chin, the way that it juts out. She could rest a coffee cup on it, it's that big and what does that say about me? Am I that ugly that he has to go with her, someone as repulsive as her?" She rummaged around in her pocket for another tissue and ferociously scrubbed her cheeks where her mascara had left black streaks. She checked herself out in the mirror and saw that her eyes were red and swollen from crying.

They turned into the street where the bank was and pulled up into the car park. It looked as though mass hysteria had happened. There was a fire truck, two ambulances, three police cars, a crowd of onlookers and a TV reporter who had just begun his live feed.

"Oh my god! What's happened?" Serena yelled to her sister as they both frantically unbuckled their seat belts and raced out of the car and over to the commotion.

"Dawn, Serena," a frail voice came from the back of the ambulance.

"Mom!" Dawn cried at her.

"Mom, what's happened, what's going on, are you okay?" Serena asked, looking her mother over for any signs of injury.

The paramedic, who had been attending to their mother, hopped into the back of the ambulance. "She's fine, ladies. She's just had a bit of an exciting day, haven't you, Martha?" he joked and winked at her.

When Serena looked around again, she saw that the main entrance of the credit union had been completely taken out. There was glass everywhere, and when she looked beyond that, she saw that her mother's car was inside the building with the teller's desk in pieces and spread over the hood. "Mother, what did you do? Your car is inside the bank."

"It was an accident, Serena. I had just pulled up into the parking lot and without even thinking, I leaned across the seat to pick my purse up. I hadn't turned the car off and my foot slipped on the gas pedal and I shot forward, straight into the bank. I don't think I hurt anyone."

"Oh, mom," Serena sighed. She removed her sunglasses and rested them on her head.

"Serena!" Dawn shouted out. "Your eye. Jesus!"

"It's okay, don't make a fuss over it. I won the fight, okay."

"Oh my god, I forgot, it was last night, wasn't it. I was so busy throwing my laptop at Phil that I forgot all about your fight. Did you see it, mom?"

"Yes, I watched it. Mary came over and watched it with me. You gave that girls parents a right good scare when you knocked her out, I bet," her mother laughed.

"Not anywhere near as scary as this, mom," Serena replied.

"How many stitches did you get?" Dawn asked as she tried to prod Serena's brow.

Serena backed away. "Get off me, Dawn. I had medical tape, no biggy."

The police and fire crew were busy sorting out the incident. The reporter, upon noticing that Serena Ward was now in his presence, came trotting over holding his microphone and being followed by his camera guy.

21

"Serena Ward? Is that you? Yes it is you. Would you mind clarifying how you're involved in this incident?" he asked, shoving the microphone to her mouth and ordering the camera guy to film her.

Serena looked at her mother, then her sister, then back at the reporter. "Well I suppose you're going to find out anyway. This is my mother, she's the one who had the accident."

"Oh, were you involved in the accident yourself?" he asked.

"No, I just arrived with my sister, after receiving a call about it. Now if you'll excuse me, I had better get back to my mom."

"Oh, right, thank you," he replied, then looked directly into the camera. "And there you have it, champion fighter Serena Ward's mother, trying to deposit her car—Cut!"

Serena sat with her mother in the back of the ambulance. Her mother, feeling extremely embarrassed, shook her head constantly.

"I'm sorry, dear, I should have been more alert. It was a stupid mistake," her mother told her.

Serena patted her mom's knee. "At least you're safe, mom, that's all that matters."

A police officer approached them and informed Serena's mother that the bank was not going to press any charges against her but there would be an insurance claim. She was free to go whenever she wanted to. Her mother was relieved at this point.

"So what do we do now?" Dawn asked. She bit her fingernail, a bad habit that she had always done as a child when she was nervous about something.

"I just want to go home," their mother said pathetically.

Serena's phone vibrated in her front pocket. She pulled it out to see that Holly was calling her. She excused herself from the others and walked over to Dawns car, where she leant up against the side of it and answered the call.

"Hi," she answered with no emotion.

'I'm sorry," Holly said.

"Me too. I should have been a little more patient with you," Serena said humbly. "Where did you drive off to?"

'I drove around for a while... nowhere special.'

"Where are you now?" Serena asked her, looking over the top of the car to see what was going on with her mother and sister.

'I'm at the gym. I've been training with Topher. He's been really good about getting me back into shape.'

"So that's it, then. Holly can chop and change her mind with the snap of her fingers and just forget about everything that we had planned out for our future." Serena snapped at her.

'This wasn't something that I just thought about out of the blue, Serena. I've missed being in shape, I've missed the training and the competing, do you not get that?'

"The only thing I don't get, is to be a parent, Holly!" She ended the call sharply.

Her mother was released from the scene and she and Dawn wandered over to the car to find Serena vexed. Still leaning up against the car, she looked at them, then without a word, she opened the back door and got inside.

"I'll drive you home, mom," Dawn said.

She was a different driver when she had her mother in the car, being cautious of every other driver on the road and constantly checking the rear view mirror.

"Well I certainly would have given your father a good laugh, if nothing else," their mother said, placing her hand over her mouth to hide her smile.

Serena rolled her eyes and then stared out of the window, remaining silent for the rest of the journey.

CHAPTER THREE

Holly arrived home later that evening. Casually walking into the house, she threw her car keys down on to the hallway table and hung her purse over the end of the stair bannister. She knew that Serena would be waiting for her and that she would be in for a dressing-down.

Serena was seated on the sofa with her legs crossed, rocking the upper leg as her resentment grew. She had heard Holly enter the house and waited intolerantly for her to come into the lounge.

Holly entered cautiously. Her face was flush and she was acting a little sheepish as she seated herself down in the armchair opposite her girlfriend. Serena's eyes were open wide as she glared at her, waiting for her next explanation of bull shit.

"I can tell that you're still mad at me," Holly said, as she looked everywhere else except at Serena.

"Mad? I'm more curious as to the sudden change in you. Without even discussing with me, the fact that you no longer want to get pregnant, the fact that you NOW want to get back into fighting and the fact that you've been MIA all day."

"I haven't been missing all day. What the hell, Serena, do I have to report my whereabouts to you every five seconds? Should I have a GPS tracker on my phone so that YOU are informed at ALL times of where I am?"

"You've been very evasive over the past few months, Holly." Serena said coldly. She stopped rocking her leg and leaned forward to pick up her bottle of water from the coffee table.

Holly began to faff with her clothing. Noticing that cat hair had floated onto her lap, she immediately stood up and brushed herself down. She was doing anything that she could to avoid any eye contact with Serena.

Serena swigged her water down, her eyes watched Holly like a hawk. She knew that Holly was up to something, she just didn't know what.

Holly stopped preening her clothing and raised her eyes to meet with Serena's. "Well there's not much else to say, is there? I'm going to bed before this really gets out of hand. I shan't wish you a good-night, as I'm sure you'll be up for most of it trying to conjure up something else to argue over, no doubt." She stormed off out of the room and ran up the stairs where she entered the bedroom and dramatically slammed the door behind her.

Serena, not sure of what was happening between them and self-questioning where she went wrong in this relationship, sat on the edge of the sofa, and with her elbows rested on her knees and her head bowed down into her hands, she silently began to cry.

Sprott made his appearance and bunted up against her lower leg. He then went an made himself comfortable on the armchair that Holly had just vacated, turning around twice on the still warm cushion, before curling up and resting his head on his front paw.

•••

Serena had fallen asleep on the sofa. A slight chill wisped over her body, causing her to wake in the middle of the night. Feeling slightly groggy, she slowly sat up, rubbed her eyes, saw that Sprott was still sleeping on the chair and then went to make her way up to bed. But as soon as she got to the bottom of the stairs, she realized that she could hear Holly's voice speaking in a low tone. She waited at the bottom step, trying to make out what she was saying. There was giggling and a, 'shush don't make me laugh.' Serena tread lightly as she made her way up the staircase, listening intently to her girlfriend fraternizing with someone else. She reached the bedroom and with her hands placed on either side of the door, she pressed her ear against the wood to hear what was being said.

'Oh, Topher, behave yourself. Really? Do you really think so? Now you've made me blush.' Holly giggled from the other side of the door.

Serena had had enough. She pressed down on the brass handle and opened the door, where she caught Holly sitting upright in bed, twirling her blond hair and talking on her phone. Holly inhaled loudly and threw her phone down onto the floor beside the bed. Guilt was written all over her face.

Serena walked into the room, her breathing was heavy with indignation as deep down she knew what Holly was up to.

"Who were you talking to, Holly?" she asked with her arms now folded across her chest.

"No-one, and why are you sneaking around in the middle of the night like that?" Holly replied trying to defend her actions.

"I'm not the one who's being sneaky, Holly. Just tell me the truth, for god sake, am I being played or not?"

Holly, looking guilty as charged, glanced at her phone that was now in two pieces on the wooden floor, then at Serena. She then glanced out of the window, then at the bed and brushed her hand over Serena's pillow. She bowed her head and nodded.

Serena, feeling heartbroken, didn't want to give Holly the satisfaction of seeing her breakdown, so she kept her emotions at bay whilst she opted to interrogate her instead. "Who is she? Do I know her?"

Holly shook her head. "It's not a she," she mumbled.

The worst thing that Holly could have ever done to Serena, was betray her with a man. Just the thought of some random guy fucking her girlfriend made Serena want to punch in the wall.

"You went with a guy?" Serena asked quietly. She was now controlling her breathing and taking her mind to a good place so that she wouldn't feel the urge to lose control over her actions and break the shit out of everything.

"Yes." Holly, who was now sobbing with her hands clasped over her face, jumped out of bed. She picked up her broken phone and thinking irrationally, she blurted out what was now on her mind. "Now I have to get a new phone."

"You heartless piece of shit, Holly!" Serena said, gritting her teeth. "You've changed so much, I hardly recognise you anymore."

"Well you won't have to put up with me any longer. I'm moving out," Holly snapped.

Serena headed for the door and looked back at Holly with eyes that were dead of any emotions. "Good, and Sprott stays with me!"

"Whatever!" Holly said, now rummaging through the wardrobe and throwing her clothing onto the bed.

Serena stayed awake for the rest of the night. Staring at blank TV screen, she played out in her mind the history of her relationship with Holly. The night that they had met was at a fight they had gone to watch and had sat next to each other. They bonded quickly over the next few days and the night that they decided to become a couple, was when they were in Serena's car, parked outside of the local college and discussing what they wanted in life. During their discussion, they noticed a stray cat run out into the road and a car driving past them hit it. Serena immediately got out of the car and picked the limp animal up. They drove straight to the veterinarians and paid for him to be operated on. After no one claimed him, they adopted him and kept him as an indoor cat, a decision that was made for his safety, as he was now partially blind.

Then she remembered the day that Holly moved in with her. That was the happiest day of her life. She had won her first fight the night before and then Holly won her fight on that afternoon. Whilst they were out celebrating, they realized that they wanted to be together for the rest of their lives. Holly moved in that evening.

Then she thought about the decision for them to become a family. Holly had been pushing to have a baby and they had saved enough money to pay for artificial insemination. Serena had supported Holly's decision to stop fighting and to get into shape for motherhood. But every month, Holly got her period.

Serena was now beginning to see where the cracks in their relationship had evolved.

•••

Serena stood at the kitchen sink sipping her coffee. She stared out of the window, once again, watching Rhonda take her little dog for his walk. The front door slammed and then she saw Holly struggling to drag a large suitcase over the red lava rocks and then to her car, where she shoved it into the trunk. She then searched through the keys on her key ring, whipped off the house key and threw it down onto the driveway. She looked at Serena, then got into her car and sped off down the street, screeching the tires and leaving tracks where they had spun. Rhonda picked her dog up and cradle him in her arms, frightened that he might have been hurt by her irresponsible driving.

Later that day Serena had gone to the training gym. She was wearing a vest top and shorts and kitted out in her boxing shoes and bag gloves and punching the heavy bag with right and left jabs and uppercuts. With each punch, she exhaled, concentrating on her movements.

"Whoa, Serena, you're really going for it today, aren't you?" Pete said as he approached her from behind. He was her trainer of many years and Serena trusted his rigorous training tactics completely.

Serena stopped punching the bag and stared at him. "I have my reasons." She then continued to jab the bag.

Pete held the bag for her to punch into. "I'd have thought that you'd be celebrating another win and on cloud nine. What's happened to make you this angry?"

"Life!" she snapped and continued to punch.

"Then let's keep this aggression for the ring, shall we." he told her firmly.

Serena chose to ignore him. She moved away from the heavy bag and sat down on the bench that was against the wall. She removed her bag gloves and unwrapped the red gauze that protected her hands. She then got on an exercise bike and began to pedal for her cool-down. After five minutes she did her stretches.

A training session was underway in the ring and two young men who were new to the club, began to spar. Serena watched them for a while, studying their imperfections from lack of experience.

Pete stood at her side. "Like what you see?" he asked as he watched along with her.

"No, not really. They're males, males suck." She turned away but before she could walk off, Pete grabbed her arm, forcing her to stay.

"Whatever it is that's eating you, make sure that it doesn't affect your status," he said.

"Fuck off, Pete, what would you know anyway?" she snapped. She yanked her arm away from his grip.

Pete waved his hands out and shook his head. "I spoke to Ricky this morning. He's setting up another fight for you."

"Good, let's hope it's soon!" she said walking away.

"It'll be a re-match between you and Wildcat. She never could accept that you were better than her," he called after her.

Serena heard him but as she was just about to enter the locker room, her pace came to a sudden halt when she heard the name, 'Topher' being called out by one of the inexperienced fighters. She turned and saw a well-toned muscular built trainer standing against the ring ropes. His body looked as though it was about to burst out his t-shirt, he was that ripped. He was telling them how move and where their faults were. He quickly glanced at her and then back to his students. Serena wasn't sure that he knew who she was but he would be a fool if he didn't. She stormed off to the locker room and got the hell out of there quickly.

The following day, she was woken by her sister banging urgently on her front door. She jumped out of bed and ran down the stairs to open the door.

"What's happened, is it mom, is she okay?" she fired at Dawn.

Dawn raced inside and headed directly into the lounge, holding a laptop close to her chest. "No, mom's fine, but you've gotta look at this." She planted the laptop down on the coffee table and started it up. "I've got him, I've got the bastard and I'm going to take him for every cent that he's got," she bellowed.

Serena sat on the sofa and watched her sister rapidly click on emails and open them up.

"Read it, go on. Just read, they're Phil's emails. He's been sending them to stick thin Cynthia. He's been planning on leaving me for months, now. What a sleaze. He's even been transferring funds from our bank account into a new one that he's opened but the dumb shit left his passwords in his desk top drawer. I have transferred every cent back into our account and opened a new one up in my name and transferred it all into that. He'll never find my

33

passwords. Ha!" She stood triumphantly with her hands on her hips and shaking her hair back behind her shoulders as though she had just won the biggest fight of her life.

Serena read the emails. Most of them referred to his love for Cynthia and she had reciprocated her feelings for him. They had even found a house to rent together.

Serena looked up at her sister. "Does he know that you have his laptop?"

"He probably does now. I've also forwarded them on to my lawyer as evidence of his affair."

Serena sat back into the sofa and sighed loudly. "I wish I'd been as alert as you for the past few months."

Dawn, confused by her remark, frowned. "Why, what possible reason could you have for a snoop like me?"

Serena rubbed her forehead. "It's Holly. I'm done with her. We broke up because she was seeing a guy behind my back."

"Holly? Nooo. Really?" She sat down on the sofa next to Serena.

"Yes, really."

"But I thought that you two were so in love and trying for a baby."

"So did I. Only she's been trying it the old fashioned way."

Dawn put her arm around her sister and comforted her. "How ironic that we're both going through this humiliation at the same time."

Serena placed her arm around Dawn's back, closed her eyes and cried like a small child. This encouraged Dawn to do the same and the pair were inconsolable.

The sun began to rise over the house, causing the shade to disappear from the back yard. Now that it was pleasantly sunny, Dawn decided to make a healthy lunch of salad and cheese and eggs. She found a cake in the back of the fridge and brought that out too and set up a table outside under the parasol for them to sit down and eat at.

She looked around at the setting and noticed how bland Serena's taste was in her décor choices. "Do you use it much?" she asked looking down at the swimming pool.

"Yes, I would normally swim in it every day but I've avoided going in over the past few days until my eye is fully healed."

"Oh, well would you mind if I borrowed one of you bikini's and had a swim later?" she asked in a childlike manner.

"Go ahead and be my guest."

Serena picked at her food whereas Dawn shovelled hers down along with a couple of glasses of white wine. She then tucked into a large slice of the cake that she had found. With her mouth full of sponge and cream, she asked

ng Gloves
Shiralyn J. Lee

Serena if she wanted a slice. Serena shook her head and
carried on picking at her food.

"You know you have to eat, right? I mean if you're in
training, that rabbit food isn't going to build you up. Come
on, eat those eggs I boiled for you." Dawn told her as she
prodded an egg with her fork and dropped it on to Serena's
plate.

"Hey, that's got cake on it," she said wiping the outer
part of the egg.

"It's cake! Who doesn't like cake?" Dawn replied with
another mouthful. Her phone rang inside her bag and when
she looked at it, she saw it was Phil calling. She left it to go
into voicemail before listening to what he had to say to her.
After giving it enough time, she clicked on to voicemail.
'What the hell, Dawny, where is my laptop? I need it, can
you give me a ring back as soon as you get this message.'

"I hate when he calls you that. 'Dawny' I mean
seriously, how old are you?" Serena voiced.

"He started calling me that when we first met. I thought
it was kind of cute but he has hardly used that nick name
lately and to hear him say it now, well, is almost
condescending, like he's trying to hide something from
me."

"Well, let's hope he has a good divorce lawyer," Serena
said.

"Let's hope he doesn't," Dawn sniggered.

With the sun now fully shining over the back yard, Dawn was swimming the length of the pool and Serena was relaxed on the wooden lounger and going through her fan mail on her tablet. Neither of them had heard Ricky enter the house.

"Hey, Serena, I rang the doorbell before I entered," he said as he came walking out through the patio door behind Serena.

Serena jolted when she heard his voice. "Shit, Ricky, you frightened me."

He kissed her forehead and sat in the lounger next to her. Seeing that there was food and drink on the table, he got up and helped himself to some snacks and poured the wine into Dawn's empty glass.

"I hope you haven't been drinking this," he asked.

"No! I have," Dawn said as she popped her head up from the poolside at Ricky's feet.

He looked down at her and seeing her in a bikini made him smile. "Dawn, wow, I haven't seen you around for a while."

She got out of the pool, the water dripped from the tiny pieces of material as typically she had worn the smallest set that she could find. She adjusted the bra top over her boobs to ensure her cleavage was showing at its best. "Nice to see you again, Ricky," she said and then wrung her wet hair out.

Ricky was smitten with Dawn. He had always liked her and when she got married, he considered it to be the worst day of his life. He still did even now. "Dawn—" He stared at her chest and her belly and his eyes almost popped out of his head when he saw how tiny her bikini bottom was, especially when she turned around to reveal that she was wearing a G-string. He tugged at the collar of his shirt to loosen it.

"Back to me, Ricky, back to me," Serena said, interrupting Ricky's obviously dirty thoughts.

"Oh, yeah, of course," he said. "Pete and I talked."

"Yeah, Pete already told me. You're setting up a re-match with Wildcat."

"So you're okay with that, then?" he asked. "And where's the lovely Holly, always as pleasant as ever Holly," he said, drumming his fingers on the patio table and looking over his shoulder to see if she was going to walk out of the house at any second.

"You never did like her, did you, Ricky?" Serena asked him.

"Hum, oh," Ricky replied as he caught site of Dawn rubbing her legs down with sun tan lotion. "Oh, Holly, no, never, I mean, I've never said that, have I?"

"You can say whatever you like about her now, she's gone. Serena kicked her out," Dawn informed him.

"Oh, really? You mean that the two of you are no longer?" Instead of simply using the word, 'together' he mimicked what he thought was an accurate account of two women together by merging his fingers together in a pecking motion.

"For god sake, Ricky. No, we're no longer doing anything," Serena scorned him.

"I was just trying to be polite. With all this political correctness, I never know where I am anymore," he said to her apologetically.

"She didn't mean to snap at you, Ricky. She kicked Holly out because she was seeing a guy. It's over between them. Now how would you like to put some lotion on my back?" Dawn teased him.

Ricky jumped at the chance and grabbed the bottle from her hand, sat on the edge of her lounger and slathered the lotion over her back whilst she lay on her front with her bikini top untied.

"You two need to get a room," Serena moaned.

"I wish," Ricky said lightheartedly and continued to massage the lotion in.

Dawn slapped his leg jokingly. Ricky liked it.

CHAPTER FOUR

Serena was at the boxing club, training for her next fight. Pete was giving her a gruelling training session and constantly told her that she could do better, even though he knew that she was doing better than her best. Ricky was encouraging her from afar, as he knew that she hated it when he would interrupt the session to ask her how she was feeling, or that he had a possible fight lined up with another opponent. It was a bad habit of his that she made him perfectly aware of.

Serena was punching the heavy bag, concentrating mainly on her uppercut punches, as Wildcat was at a height advantage on her. She knew that this girl was good and in the last match, she gave it her all to try and beat Serena. With this being said, Serena was determined to keep her reign as champion.

It was unlike Ricky to fall silent during her training session and when she noticed that there was a deafening silence, she turned to see why he had stopped talking. Her heart fell to her feet when she realized the reason.

Holly and her so called boyfriend had just entered the club. Holly gave a snide side glance to Serena as she walked by to get to the locker room.

"Just ignore them," Pete told her. "Now, 40 overheads," he said, still holding the heavy bag.

Serena punched into that bag with so much force. Her shoulder muscles were ripped, her biceps, ripped and her stomach muscles ripped. Her thighs and calf's were solid. She had never looked physically better.

The gossip had spread around the club about her and Holly and she could see other members nudging each other and whispering, thinking that she wouldn't notice them doing it. This annoyed Serena and she imagined Holly's face on the bag as she punched it one final time.

"Great, Serena, now go and do your cool down," Pete told her.

He walked away and looking at Ricky, he shook his head in disapproval of the two show offs who had just entered.

"If anyone's going to bring down that girl, it's those two over there," he said to Ricky. "Serena needs to clear her mind and forget about Holly if she wants to continue her reign as champion."

With his finger stuck in his mouth, picking at the back of his front teeth, Ricky stood and stared at the pair and then turned to look at Serena. "Hum."

With her back facing her ex-girlfriend, Serena stretched to cool down. Pete walked over to her and patted her on her back and told her that she had done a great training session. She then had to walk past Holly and Topher to get to the locker room. She held her head high and kept her eyes focused in front of her as she marched past.

Holly attempted to say something to her but Topher prevented her by pulling her arm back and using his eye contact with her to show his disapproval. Serena smiled as she had seen his jealous reaction through the corner of her eye.

After she had showered and dressed, she re-entered the gym area to say goodbye to Ricky and Pete. They were involved in a deep conversation in Pete's office. The door was closed, which meant, 'Keep out!' Serena hung around for a few minutes but then her attention was drawn to the ring. Inside the ropes, Holly was training with a sparring partner. Serena watched her, monitoring her moves with great detail. It had been a while since Holly had been in training, or at least, since Serena had seen her.

She looked good, her jabs needed a little work but overall, she was turning out to be a good fighting contender.

"Hey, got a problem?" Topher shouted at Serena.

Holly stopped sparring to see why he was shouting.

"No! And what's it to do with you?" Serena shouted back.

"Holly! Get back to it," he demanded.

"Jesus, what a dick," Serena muttered under her breath.

Pete and Ricky emerged from the office to see what the shouting was all about. Pete hadn't been too keen to keep

Holly on as member but Topher had pushed for it and Topher had money to bribe Pete with.

"Hey, what's all the shouting about?" Pete called to Topher.

"Intimidation toward my client. Checking out competitive moves. You name it. I want her kept away from us," Topher said loudly so that everyone could hear his complaint.

Ricky took Serena by her arm and led her out of the building before any more trouble erupted.

Out in the car park Ricky apologized to Serena for acting so swiftly in removing her from the club. He had had dealings with Topher in the past and knew that he wasn't a team player when it came to the crunch. He'd also just been told by Pete that Topher had requested that Serena stayed away from the club due to the indifferences between her and Holly. He also made it clear that he would help Pete pay some debts off. Pete refused his offer when it came to Serena. If anyone was going to leave, it would be Holly.

"I have every right to train here, Ricky. Just who the hell do they think they are? Holly isn't even capable of entering competitions yet, she's been out of action for far too long. She'll need to train for months to get back to where she was."

"Apparently, she's been in training for months from what Topher told Pete," Ricky told her.

"What? Wait. How could she have been? She's been at home trying to conceive our baby. Why the hell would you say that, Ricky?"

"Because it's true. Why do you think she hasn't been attending your fights? Where did you think she was going every time she left the house after your arguments? Straight to Topher for training, that's where."

"That lying bitch!" Serena screamed.

"I only found this all out a few minutes ago from Pete. Apparently he had no knowledge that Topher was using his gym late at night when it was closed. Topher is paying him quite a lot for his services in the club. Hey, I need you to keep it for the ring. Use that anger against your opponent," he told her.

"Yeah, right. Easy for you to say," she snapped. Her phone vibrated in her pocket. It was her mother calling.

'Hi, sweetheart, just calling to see how that eye of yours is,' she said.

"Mom, I can't talk right now, can I call you back later?"

'Yes, sure dear.'

Serena put her phone back into her pocket. "Shit, just shit, Ricky." She got into her car and sped off down the street.

The lights had turned red and Serena sat waiting for them to change. She watched the traffic flow from the cross street and waited some more. She now found her fingers tapping erratically on the steering wheel, then she beeped the car horn, showing her impatience. "Jesus, Dawn was right."

Arriving home and slamming the car door, Serena waved at Rhonda who was watching her out of her kitchen window. She then entered her house, threw down her gear and sauntered off to the kitchen. Sprott came running in and as usual, gave a loud meow to let her know he was hungry, even though he still had a bowl of kibble, he would always demand a feast of meat at least twice a day. He wrapped himself around her lower legs until she opened the can and emptied it into his bowl, then he left her alone so he could eat.

She opened the fridge door and grabbed the milk, opened it and drank straight from the carton. She then remembered to call her mom.

"Hey, mom, sorry about earlier. I had some issue to deal with. How are you, anyway?"

'I'm okay, dear. I was more concerned about you. How's your eye, I hope it's cleared up now?'

"Yeah, it's okay, mom. The bruising is coming out now."

'I had a phone call this morning from Holly. She said that she wanted to say goodbye as she always had a soft spot for me. What happened between the two of you?'

"Oh, mom. I can't go into it right now but I do know that she meant well in calling you. We just happened to grow apart."

'Well I'm really sorry to hear that, dear. Now you take care of yourself and we'll meet up soon.'

"Okay, mom, take care."

'Bye, dear.'

"Bye, mom."

•••

The weeks counted down and tonight was the fight between Viper Girl and Wildcat. The build-up had been posted on all social networks, tickets were sold out and Viper Girl was fighting fit and ready to take out her challenger.

Dawn and her mother had ringside seats and were eagerly awaiting to watch Serena in action.

Serena was in the locker room. Ricky was pumping her with what she had to gain from winning this fight and Pete was feeding her with encouragement. They were called for the weigh in and Viper Girl weighed in at 135lb Wildcat weighed in at 134lb.

Back in the dressing room, Viper Girl's hands were wrapped in gauze and taped in front of the commission. Then her gloves were placed on her hands and she was on her way through the hallway and out into the stadium. The crowd were showing overwhelming support by screaming and shouting out Viper Girls name. She was their favorite fighter and all bets were on her to win.

Wildcat emerged into the stadium and still the crowd cheered but not as loudly as for the previous fighter.

Viper Girl climbed into the ring and sat on a stool in her corner. Wildcat sat in her corner. Ricky and Pete both gave Viper Girl the low-down on her opponent, then Ricky jumped down out of the ring but remained close by.

"Remember, Wildcat's weakness is no longer her height. She'll be expecting you to throw a few uppercuts," Pete informed her. "Make sure you pack all of your bodyweight into the punches. Seize your chance quickly, okay."

"Yep." She placed her mouth guard in and stood up ready to fight. She jabbed the air, putting on a show for her fans. Her style of fighting was 'Swarmer' normally known as an 'in-fighter.' She was fast with her floods of 'hooks' and 'upper-cuts' and was able to receive many jabs to her own body without it affecting her performance. Her shorter height actually gave her an advantage over her opponent as she had the ability to get in close and cause her opponent to find it harder to throw a punch at close reach.

Wildcat was an out-fighter. Her ability to maintain distance between her and her opponent gave her the advantage of longer reach jabs. She was able to control the pace of the fight and was capable of leading her opponent. Her punches were fast and she had good hand speed and footwork and Viper Girl knew this.

The referee signalled for the first round to start and both fighters moved from their assigned corners toward each other. Wildcat was the first to throw a jab but Viper Girl was able to bob, and weaved to the side to avoid contact. The two fighters circled and again, Wildcat was able to throw a punch, this time managing to catch Viper Girl on the chin. Viper Girl clinched on to Wildcat, the referee intervened and shouted, 'Break,' both fighters took a step back from each other.

They stepped toward each other again and circled, Wildcat threw another jab but Viper Girl was ready and tucked herself inside, and using the force of her bodyweight, she threw out an uppercut punch to Wildcat's chin but Wildcat counteracted with an attempted hook to the side of Viper Girl's head but Viper Girl used a parry block, causing Wildcat to hit the upper palm of her glove, Wildcat retracted her fists quickly, both fighters circled with their fists in front of their faces.

The referee signalled the end of round one and both fighters went to their assigned corners. Viper Girl sat on her stool and Pete jumped up through the ropes, removed her mouth guard and fed her water, then rubbed her shoulders. He gave her a pep talk on her faults and told her where she needed to concentrate. He checked her over for any signs of injury and then the referee signalled for round two to start.

Both opponents left their corners and round two began. Immediately, transferring her weight from her rear foot to her lead foot, Viper Girl, with her left hand below her chin, threw out a powerful cross. She retracted her hand quickly and resumed the guard position and then, rotating her hips, she sent out a hook, hitting her target directly at the side of her head. Wildcat's legs gave way and she fell to the ground. The referee began his count to ten.

The crowded audience cheered and screamed for Viper Girl to win.

Serena's mom stood up and cupped her mouth. "Go, Viper Girl!" she shouted and sat back down. She looked at Dawn and leant into her. "She's got this in the bag."

Dawn, with her eyes still on the ring and watching the countdown, replied, "I think she does, mom."

The referee counted, whilst Wildcat remained motionless on the ground. "1,2,3,4,5,6,7,8,9,10." He bent down and removed her mouth guard, then her cutman and trainer came bounding into the ring.

Pete and Ricky jumped into the ring and ran over to Viper Girl. Pete lifted her up. She punched her fists into the air, marking her victory.

The judges scored the fight in favor of Viper Girl, resulting in round one 10-10 and round two a knockdown, 10-8.

"You did it, you fucking did it," Ricky roared at her.

Serena spat her mouth guard out and looked over to her mom and sister. Shaking her fists triumphantly, she let out a, "Hell, yeah!"

Dawn stood up and turned to the crowd and self-importantly shouted, "That's my sister."

Viper Girl and her entourage paraded through the stadium, high-fiving her fans, signing autographs and basically feeling proud of her success. Ricky constantly patted her on her back.

•••

Serena was the center of attention in the locker room. Her mother, her sister, Ricky, Pete and a few other members who had invested their money in her, were all in celebratory mode. Ricky offered to treat everyone to drinks at his favorite jaunt, later on.

During the interview, Viper Girl sat in between Ricky and Pete.

"How does it feel to still be the reigning champion, Viper Girl?" one reporter asked.

"It feels like I chose the right profession," Viper Girl replied.

Subtle laughter filled the room.

"So will you be remaining under Ricky Koch's management?" another reporter asked.

"Oh, most definitely. We go back a long way and we work well together. Ricky's got my back, I'm sure of it," she replied.

Ricky jokingly patted her back.

50

"Do you think that fight was your personal best?"

"I always think that and then I fight again and think that fight was. It never ends. I'll always strive to be better in the next fight."

"Serena, where do you see yourself going from here?"

"To the locker room just down the hallway," she smiled. "But seriously, I do need to get changed."

Ricky and Pete stood up first, prompting the end of the interview.

After changing into her jeans and t-shirt, Serena, Dawn and their mother got into Serena's car and followed Ricky and Pete in his Porsche, down the highway, heading for the pub.

Serena had decided to drive being as she hadn't been hurt in the fight. Dawn sat in the passenger seat next to her and their mother sat in the back seat behind Serena. Dawn pressed the button to open the window.

"Could you close it a bit, please Dawn, it's a bit blustery back here?" her mother asked her.

"Oh, yeah, sure mom, I didn't think," she replied. She pressed the button to do the window up a bit. A small gray spider had crawled over the wing mirror and then into the car and along the inside top of the door. Dawn, who was normally paranoid about spiders, wanted to show how brave she was and looked inside her purse for something to use to knock the spider away. Finding a credit card, she flicked the spider out of the window and pressed the button to close the window fully, thinking that she had rid herself of the problem.

Serena looked across to see what she was doing. "Did you get rid of it? I thought I saw it on the door."

Dawn, feeling proud answered back, "Oh no, it's outside, I witnessed it myself."

Serena kept looking over at Dawn's door. Dawn, beginning to feel unnerved, double checked the door and re-confirmed that there was nothing there. In the meantime, they were now driving at a speed 80kms and just merged onto a bridge. Then, something caught Dawn's attention when it moved on the door. Dawn was horrified that the spider had somehow re-entered the car without her seeing it. The spider was fast and crawled straight toward her. Dawn, feeling extremely frazzled, lifted up out of her seat and with her seat belt still on, she veered her body toward Serena. The spider crawled fast and was gunning for her. Dawn panicked and in the moment of disturbance, she unbuckled her seat belt, screamed and slipped her body in between the driver and passenger seat, forcing herself onto the back seat, narrowly missing her mother. Breathing heavy and sweating profusely, she buckled herself into the rear seat belt. Serena had had to remain calm during this escaped. Dawn was now in a state of panic and looked everywhere for the spider. She lifted her feet up and scoured the side of the car and the carpet below.

"Dawn, you need to calm down," Serena said.

"It's just a little spider," her mother said, shaking her head at the performance that her daughter was now creating.

Just then Dawn looked to her side and saw the spider run along the back seat and underneath her. She screamed the loudest scream that she had ever let out. She unfastened her seat belt and threw herself onto her mother's lap.

"Stop the car, Serena, stop the god damn car," she screamed.

Serena pulled the car over on the side of the road. She got out of the car and immediately following her, Dawn pushed the driver seat forward and jumped out of the car, still screaming.

"Jesus, Dawn, it's just a spider, deal with it."

"I'm not getting back into that car until you've found it and thrown it far away," she said brushing herself down and feeling as though she was now being violated by creepy crawlies.

Serena lent into the car through the passenger side. "Mom, are you all right?"

"Oh sure dear. I'm having fun watching the pair of you react to a wee spider," she said with her hands on her lap and smiling at the pair.

"I'm not the one who's reacting like a girl!" Serena clearly stated.

"Is it gone, have you got it yet?" Dawn asked pathetically whilst trying to peek over Serena's shoulder.

Serena searched the interior of the car, then pushed the seat forward to find the creature running along the carpet. Reacting quickly, she pulled out a piece of paper from her jacket pocket and scooped the spider up and flicked it out to the ground. Dawn screamed and in a frenzy, ran around to the other side of the car, hopping from one foot to the other in case it came searching for her.

"Really, Dawn?" Serena asked her as she pushed the seat back into its original position.

"I'm not going back around there— I'll drive!" she said, panicking that it might still be there. She jumped into the driver's seat and whipped on the seat belt, constantly looking around for anything that was moving.

Serena flapped her arms, then got into the car. Shaking her head, she fastened her seat belt.

"You can drop me off at home, girls. I think I've had enough excitement for one evening," their mother said.

"Are you sure, mom?" Serena asked.

"Quite sure, dear," she replied.

Dawn drove them to their mother's house which was just around the corner from the pub. All three got out of the car.

"I'm so very proud of you, Serena. Even though I hate that you get hurt, I can't bear to see that happen to you but you are very good at what you do. Dawn! I love you. I love you both, now go and enjoy yourselves," their mother said. She gave them both a hug and went inside her house.

They waited in the car until she was safely inside and waved to them from the window.

"I have a question to ask you," Dawn said as they drove away.

"Yeah, what is it?"

"I have an appointment tomorrow with Edmund Harding, he's my divorce lawyer. Apparently we're sitting down with Phil and his lawyer to discuss who gets what. Would you come along with me, just for moral support?"

"Of course I will, Dawn. How are things between you two? Have you spoken at all?"

"Hell no! If he wants to contact me, he will have to do it through my lawyer. He's already tried to claim back the money he transferred from our bank account. Seriously, he thinks that my hard earned wages should pay toward his love nest with that stick."

"So do you know how long their affair had been going on for?"

"His emails gave him away. I would say they had been getting it on for at least five months. I noticed he'd changed toward me at around the same time, he was staying out late, not even looking at me like he used to and as for sex— well, I suppose you understand what I mean about that."

Serena glanced at her with one eyebrow raised. "One thing about Holly, I never had a clue that she was double dipping on me. She had changed, yeah, but I put it all down to not getting pregnant."

"I bet you're glad that it didn't get that far, sheesh, just imagine the court battle you'd have on your hands now."

"I don't even want to think about it," Serena said as they pulled up into the car park.

CHAPTER FIVE

Dawn walked into the pub first closely followed by Serena. A loud cheer came from the bar area and flurries of congratulations came their way. Serena took a bow and thanked everyone. Ricky and Pete were seated at the long mahogany bar and had ordered some beers. They'd kept a couple of bar stools free for Selena and Dawn.

Ricky picked up one of the bottles of beer and showed it to Serena as a gesture for her to drink. "A beer for the most sought after champion?"

She took it from him and sat in one of the stools. He then picked up another and passed it to Dawn. "And one for such a beautiful lady."

"Why thank you," she said and sat in between her sister and Ricky.

There was a row of four flat screen TVs running above the back of the bar and Ricky had persuaded the barman to play a DVD of the fight. They watched the match and swigged back beer with everyone in the pub cheering.

Pete held out his bottle, pointing the end of it toward Serena, he smiled. "Cheers," he said.

Serena copied his act, "Cheers, Pete."

Ricky, feeling his chances were in, placed his hand onto Dawn's shoulder as he flirted with her. She didn't mind, in fact, she was enjoying the attention. Serena just shook her head.

A woman with long auburn curly hair and in her mid-twenties had walked in through the main entrance. She gripped tightly to the handle of her purse as it hung over her shoulder. Her eyes scoured the room until they met with Ricky's. He nodded his head, she nodded back. He then lent back behind Dawn and wagged his finger in Serena's direction. The woman acknowledged him and then approached Serena at the bar.

She positioned herself between Serena and a man who was sat in the next bar stool and leaned forward, pretending to try to attract the bartender's attention.

Her perfume was alluring to Serena, who didn't miss the opportunity to take a glance at the woman's cleavage, not that Serena was being a pervert, it was just that the woman had chosen to wear a black mini halter-neck dress that the front bodice veered down past her breasts and met at the waistline. There were a lot more eyes on this woman but she had chosen to be appealing to Serena.

"Here, have one of these," Serena said to her as she passed a bottle of beer to her. "You'll be waiting a while to get served, have this on me."

The woman, with her arms rested on the bar, smiled at Serena. She accepted the beer and chinked the opened bottle with Serena's bottle. She brushed her hair back behind her ear, revealing large gold hooped earrings. "Cheers," she said softly.

Serena looked around to see if anyone was with this woman. "Are you on your own?"

The woman pushed herself away from the bar and turned to face Serena. "You could say that." She swigged her beer from the bottle and then placed it down on the bar. "I'm Raquel but you can call me anything you like tonight."

"Well Raquel, thank you for that but I'm not really looking for anything—"

"Shush." Raquel placed her finger over her mouth. She leaned in close to Serena and whispered into her ear. "Your friend has paid for my services for the entire night, you really can call me anything you like."

Serena reeled back slightly. "My friend?"

Raquel looked beyond Serena and over to Ricky. Serena followed her gaze and turned to look at Ricky who lifted his beer and mouthed the words, 'You're welcome.'

Serena jumped off her stool and stood right in front of Ricky. "You hired a fucking prostitute for me. Are you insane, Ricky?"

"You haven't been laid in weeks, Serena. Let's face it, being around you over the past few weeks has not been that pleasant at all," he said.

"Pete, did you know anything about this?" Serena asked him.

He held his hands up and laughed. "I had nothing to do with it," he said.

Dawn looked at Serena, then at Ricky, then at Pete and back to Serena. "What's going on, have I missed something?"

Serena smacked her beer down on the bar and looked directly at her sister. "Ricky hired a prostitute. He thought that I might need a good seeing to."

Dawn, not quite understanding her sister's dilemma, laughed. "Don't be silly, a prostitute, really."

"Yes, really, Dawn!"

Raquel raised her hand and waved politely. "Bought and paid for."

Ricky, dangling a door key in the air, leaned into Serena's shoulder. "This is the hotel room key. What have you got to lose?"

•••

Raquel closed the drapes, pulled the bed sheets down the bed and then untied her halter-neck dress, allowing it to fall to her feet. She stepped out of it and now wearing just her panties and high-heels, she stood with her hands on her hips, showing off her valuable assets. Serena jumped onto the bed and laying on her back, she admired Raquel's slender body.

"Like what you see?" Raquel asked, her voice sultry.

"A huh," Serena murmured and nodded.

Raquel approached the edge of the bed and grabbed Serena's runners. She tugged them and pulled them off her feet. She then removed her socks. Serena, relaxed, watched her. Raquel then proceeded to run her hands over Serena's legs and made her way up to the brass button on her jeans waistband. She popped it through the eyelet and prised them open. Serena lifted her butt and Raquel pulled the jeans down her legs and cast them onto the navy blue rug at the foot of the bed.

Serena, resting on her elbows, gave her a wry smile.

Raquel then straddled herself over Serena's thighs and ran her hands below her t-shirt, running her fingers up over Serena's taught stomach and firm breasts. She slipped the t-shirt up over her head and threw it down on the floor behind her. She then pushed Serena back down onto the mattress and planted a kiss on her neck, working her way down Serena's throat and over her shoulder. Serena began to breathe deeply, concentrating on what this woman was doing to her. She rolled her eyes back and closed them and allowed Raquel to take control of her body.

"Relax," Raquel told her. "I can tell that you're tense, I do have a dental dam if you're worried about any hygiene issues."

Serena covered her eyes with her hand. "I know, I know. It's hard for me to do this. Not that there's anything wrong with you, I mean the way you look. But my ex-girlfriend, she just trampled right over my feelings."

"Sure, I understand where you're coming from," Raquel said and carried on kissing Serena's firm chest area.

"It just feels so clinical and—"

"And what?" Raquel asked her.

"Well, dirty." Serena said, sitting up. She looked around the room and took note on how expensive it all looked. "I mean I'm here in this room and I should be doing this with someone I at least care about. No offense."

Raquel stared into Serena's eyes. "None taken," she said and then moved in to kiss Serena's cheek.

Serena began to ramble on about her and Holly and that she had always been loyal to her and her past girlfriends.

Raquel stopped what she was doing. "Have you been with a prostitute before?"

"No, no way, no, this is my first time."

"Have you ever had meaningless sex?"

"No," Serena answered softly.

Raquel gently persuaded Serena to lie back down on the bed and whilst Serena spoke of Holly and how they had met whilst watching a fight, Raquel had removed Serena's shorts and maneuvered herself in between Serena's thighs. When Serena felt the warmth of Raquel's breath followed by the tenderness of her soft tongue, she gave up conversing about her past relationship and began to enjoy the moment that she was now experiencing.

•••

The following morning Serena woke to find that Raquel had already left.

"Something I said," she joked to herself as she slipped from beneath the sheets and headed to the bathroom to take a shower. Her mood had lifted and once under the hot spray of water, she began to sing and even though she didn't know all of the words, she found herself mumbling made-up words to fill in the gaps.

After drying herself, she dressed and then ordered breakfast to be brought up to her room. She sat at a small table by the window that overlooked a busy street of shoppers and tucked into a plate of scrambled eggs and bacon. And whilst she sipped her coffee, she went through her emails and messages on her phone. She'd received a text message from Dawn telling her not to be late. Serena checked the time on her watch. It was now 10.15am.

"Shit!" she shouted, realizing that she should have already been on her way to pick Dawn up. Picking up her wallet and keys and running out of the room toward the elevator, she texted her sister back, stating that she would be there soon.

Dawn was all ready to leave. She stood at her window that overlooked the street, waiting for Serena to arrive. Seeing her car turn into the street and pull into her driveway, she picked up her purse and came rushing out of the house.

Slightly flustered, she got into the car. "Where the hell have you been? I bet he's there now with his tart and the pair of them are probably giving it their all to make me out to be the bad guy."

"We should be right on time, no more than five minutes late at the most. Now buckle up, I'll drive as fast as I can."

"I'm sorry, I'm just so on edge with all of this. It's absolutely ridiculous that I have to discuss my personal business with that 'stick' listening to it all. I bet she's already started spending my money." She opened her purse and rummaged through the contents until she drew out a lipstick. She pulled down the sun visor and monitored herself in the mirror as she layered a thick coat of deep pink over her lips. "Well at least I'm going to look stunning, which is actually more than I can say for my nemesis."

"How did he meet her?" Serena asked.

"She was a dental hygienist at his surgery. I'd say she did more than just clean teeth. I put a lot of my own money into that surgery and as a silent partner, I'll be damned if she gets a cent of my share."

"Will you sell your half?"

"Hell if I get the right offer, sure I will."

They drove into the underground car park beneath the lawyers offices. Dawn got out of the car first and wanting to maintain her best appearance, she checked her reflection out in the passenger window.

"How's my hair? She asked Serena, who was now pressing the car remote to lock it.

"Why do you keep running your hands through it? You look fine—actually, more than fine. You look amazing."

"Hey, I forgot to ask you. How did you get on last night? Was she good? Did you at least get to have an orgasm?"

"Jesus, Dawn, that's a bit personal."

"Hey, it's been a while for me too, you know. I know what it's like to go without down there. I'm starting to feel as though I may need her services too if the dry season doesn't end."

"So do I sense that you and Ricky might have a thing?"

Dawn laughed politely. "I think Ricky's cute, I won't deny that but I'm not going to drop my panties on demand for him. He can sweat it out a little, I just need to get Phil out of my life first."

They walked over to the elevator and waited for it to come to the car park floor. The doors slid open and the two stepped inside. Just as the doors were about to close, a hand reached in and pulled them open. It was Phil, dressed in his best suit and he was with Cynthia. Dawn's eyes widened as she looked at Serena and held her breath in. Phil, making a gesture to his girlfriend that everything was okay, clasped his hand into hers. She looked at him and smiled. Feeling triumphant, he glanced over his shoulder at Dawn, in return, she poked her tongue out at him.

65

"Immature behavior," he whispered.

It was a huge relief for all concerned when the elevator reached the third floor and the doors opened, allowing Serena and Dawn to separate from the happy couple. They walked down a navy blue carpeted hallway until they reached the receptionist desk. She invited them all to wait in the seated area until their respective lawyers were present. Dawn's lawyer, Hilary Mason, was the first to arrive and she offered for her and Serena to join her in the meeting room where they sat around a large glass table. He opened his brief case and pulled out a brown card file with Dawn's documents inside. He laid them down on the table and quickly revised his notes. Dawn and Serena sat silent, patiently waiting for the meeting to start.

The door opened and Phil, dressed in a dark gray suit, sheepishly walked in with Cynthia, a tall thin woman wearing a red wrap over style dress, and his lawyer, Mr. Paxton, a short, balding man wearing thick rimmed glasses. They sat on the opposite side of the table. Dawn's eyes narrowed as she glared at Cynthia. Cynthia's eye darted all over the place in order to avoid her boyfriend's wife's daggering glare.

"I'm keeping the house!" Dawn announced. Her stare was directed at Cynthia.

"May I suggest that if we want to progress forward, that we need to keep to the list of demands and go through all assets that both clients are asking for," Phil's lawyer, with his eyes peering over the top rim of his glasses, explained calmly.

Cynthia smiled to herself, an act that didn't go unnoticed by Dawn.

"Suggest what you like," Dawn interrupted again. "The house is mine. The inheritance money I received from my father paid for that house AND its contents, long before I met Phil and I think you'll find that Phil actually signed a prenuptial agreement just in case we did end up filing for a divorce. I wouldn't have married him otherwise. And by the way," she said staring at Cynthia. "I'm also your boss, something that you seemed to have overlooked. Yeah, that's right, Phil, no more silent partner for you, I'm coming to work at MY office, the one that I fifty percent own!"

"Just wait a moment here, Dawny—"

Dawn grimaced. "Don't call me Dawny!"

Cynthia, scowled at Phil, shocked that he had just used his cute pet name for his wife. "Don't call her Dawny, Phil," she spoke out.

Dawn's lawyer flicked through her notes and paperwork until she found the necessary document in question. She placed it on the table in front of Phil's lawyer and tapped her finger on his signature. He picked it up and smacking his lips together as he scoured the form, he shrugged his shoulders and passed it back.

"Ha," Dawn let out loudly. "And don't think that he'll be faithful to you for long," she directed at Cynthia. "He was living with a woman when he met me. They'd been together for more than five years but he convinced me that he wasn't happy with her and that meeting me was the best thing that had ever happened to him. Too right it was, I had money and he knew that."

Serena, who had remained silent throughout, looked confused at her sister's confession. "I didn't know that. You mean he had an affair with you while he was shacked up with some other woman?"

"I'm sure that we can do without your dirty laundry being aired," Phil's lawyer told her.

"I'm sure that I am perfectly capable of instructing my client on what to air, Mr. Paxton," Hilary informed him.

"You didn't know that, did you, Cynthia?" Dawn asked her with a smug smile across her face.

Cynthia looked at Phil, then at Dawn, her eyes were filled with questions.

"You make it sound as though I was a callous ass where in fact, if I remember quite rightly, it was you who did all the chasing. I didn't leave that relationship as easily as you portray. Anna begged me to stay with her but you just wouldn't give up. Even when Anna fell pregnant with Lucas, you still pursued me," Phil said.

"You wanted me!" Dawn retorted.

"Who's Lucas?" Serena asked.

"His son!" Dawn replied sharply.

"His son?" Cynthia asked, shocked that this was the first that she was hearing about this information.

Phil coughed. "I was going to tell you, Cynthia. I was just waiting for the right time."

Well you'll be waiting for a long time," she said getting up and pushing her chair back hard. She stormed off toward the door.

Dawn watched Cynthia walk away, delighted that she had put a spanner in the works. "Get yourself a burger while you're out, you need to put some fat on those bones, maybe some fries too and a shake."

"Really!" Cynthia huffed and then exited the room, leaving the door wide open.

Serena, feeling awkward at this point, decided that it was best for her to leave the room and let her sister sort out her affairs in private. She waited in the reception area just staring at the boring pictures on the walls and catching a smile from the receptionist.

"I know who you are now," the receptionist said. "You're Serena Ward, aren't you?"

Serena nodded at her and smiled. Her phone vibrated in her jeans pocket, it was Ricky calling her.

"Hey what's up, Ricky?"

'I've just had a very interesting conversation.'

"Well that's nice, I've had a few of those myself,"
Serena giggled.

'No, no, wait. I mean I've had a conversation with
Topher, he's hinting at the idea of you and Holly in the
ring.'

Serena stood up sharp and marched over to the window.
Pulling back the blinds and gazing down at the street
below, she took a moment to allow the information to sink
in. "What the fuck are you talking about, Ricky. I hope to
god that you said no—Ricky, you did say no, didn't you?"

'I haven't said anything either way, Serena. I told him
that I would speak with you and with Pete. You know I
don't make decisions on a whim, I like to mull things over
and think about them. I'm telling you to do the same.'

"I can tell you right now, there's no way in hell, Ricky!
For heaven's sake, she my ex-girlfriend, why the hell
would she want to do this?"

'I don't think Topher's told her yet.'

"You mean he's trying to make these decisions without
even telling her? I have to tell her, she needs to know!"

'I doubt whether you'll even get the chance to speak
with her. Topher's got her on a tight leash, literally.'

"She's not even up to my standards, she's been out of it
for too long."

70

"Who's been out of what for too long?" Dawn asked as she approached Serena.

"Ricky, I have to go, Dawn's finished her appointment with her lawyer."

'Okay, tell her I said hi.'

Serena turned around to Dawn to see Phil behind her, disappearing out of the main entrance. Dawn was smiling as if she was contented with her outcome.

"Don't you just love it when your stars are aligned?" she said wryly.

CHAPTER SIX

Serena had gone for an early run in the nearby parkland. It was a favorite place of hers because there were many shaded areas where the sun rays could be filtrated through the mass of foliage on the trees. Today was no exception. With her earphones in, she listened to her music on her phone. Her mind wasn't focused on anything in particular, just a few random considerations of no importance. But then, thoughts of Holly came flooding in and it was as if she was having a saturation of flashbacks of everything that they had done together. She stopped running, pulled out her earphones and rested up against a tree trunk. Those tingling feelings that she felt when she had first met Holly, engulfed her, causing her to self-question why she was still so emotionally attached to her.

"Shit Holly! Why, why did you have to do this to us?" she called out into the open air.

Distracting her from her thoughts was a woman who, running along the same path, had suddenly tripped and fallen into the shrubbery. Serena looked over at her to see if she was okay.

"Ouch! Shit! What the Fu—."

"Are you okay?" Serena interrupted her. She held her hand out to help the woman up.

The dishevelled woman looked up at her. Her white baseball cap and sunglasses had fallen to the ground causing her to squint as the sunlight was behind Serena. "Yes. Just my pride compromised, that's all." She grabbed Serena's hand and pulled herself up onto her feet.

"Okay, as long as you're all right." Serena turned to walk away.

"Ruth!"

"Sorry?" Serena asked, turning back.

"Ruth, my name's Ruth Jenkins. And thank you for rescuing me." She held her hand out to shake Serena's. There was a momentary pause between the two of them. "It's okay, I don't bite."

Serena, relaxed her stance, clasped Ruth's hand and shook it. "I'm Serena Ward, nice to meet you."

Ruth brushed the dirt and moss from her long brown hair and then checked the backs of her legs for any scratches. "Not a good choice to wear white," she joked at her own expense, looking down at her white vest top and capri pants that were now ruined with grass stains. "I feel like such an idiot. Please believe me that I'm not usually this accident prone. I run this route practically every day."

"Yeah? I haven't seen you around before," Serena said, motioning that they should move out of the wooded area.

"That's because I normally run in the evenings but I had to change my schedule this week."

They trekked along the dirt pathway, through the wooded area and out toward the car park at the edge of the park.

"Well I live that way, just up the hill." Serena explained to Ruth.

"Oh really?" Ruth looked toward the car park. "Well I have a confession to make. I actually drove here, not that I'm lazy or anything, it's just that I don't live close by, so driving was my only option."

"That's okay, I won't poke fun at you, I know how it is." Serena checked the time on her watch. "So, I have to go now but it really was nice meeting you. Maybe we'll see each other again, running somewhere."

"Yes, I'm sorry that I kept you. Perhaps we could meet up again. Here! Take my phone number and call me whenever you're free." She pulled out a business card from her front pocket and presented it to Serena. "Or perhaps not," she said sheepishly retracting it.

"No, it's okay. I'll take your card." She took it from Ruth's hand and looked at it. "Oh, you're an author, I see."

"Yes I am indeed. Although I write for a niche market."

"Oh yeah?"

"Don't be alarmed but I write lesbian erotica. Not too many people appreciate that genre."

Serena laughed. "I think you're safe with me. Give me another one of your cards. I'll write down where I work out

74

at. If you feel comfortable enough to hang around there, then maybe we'll have something in common." She wrote down the address to Pete's training gym on the back of Ruth's business card and handed it back to her.

"Hum, so you work out in a training gym? You mean like a boxing type of gym?" Ruth asked.

"Just come and visit me. See you there."

Serena strode away, leaving Ruth to ponder over her comment.

•••

Walking into Pete's gym, Serena headed straight for his office to speak with either him or Ricky if he was around.

Pete was at his desk talking on the phone to his ten year old daughter. Serena waited outside the door until he had finished his call.

"Serena, come in," Pete called out to her.

Serena entered and sat down on the edge of his desk. She picked up a framed photo that he had of his daughter and studied her facial features. "She looks a lot like you, Pete. I bet you miss not seeing her around as much anymore."

Pete nodded. "She has her mother's eyes though, don't you think?"

"Yeah, she does. So how is she coping in her new environment?"

"She said she's good and I think that she's excited that her mother and Gordon are getting married, she's going to be a bridesmaid."

"WOW! How do feel about that?"

"The truth? It hurts like hell but I'm not going to let it ruin my life. If Helen loves this man and Livvy sees him as a father figure, then who am I to interfere? Now come on, let's get you out there. Jenny's still here, I'll get her to spar with you."

"Cool, I get to kick Jenny's ass."

"Jenny, gear up, you can spar with Serena," Pete shouted across the room.

"Sure, Pete," Jenny replied.

Serena got into the ring, fitted her headgear and put in her mouth guard, then fastened her sparring gloves. Jenny stepped into the ring and the two initiated their sparring tactics. Pete stood at the ringside calling out Serena's best tactical moves.

"See her punches coming, Serena, work on your defense moves. Jenny, throw a jab, Serena, shift your weight," Pete called out.

Serena punched and slipped, then shifted her weight to avoid Jenny's incoming punch. They circled and then Jenny threw another jab, Serena rolled away from it.

"Good, Serena, good move!" Pete shouted. "Now set it up with your head further back, Jenny, I want you to throw a long shot. Try to land it hard."

Serena followed his instructions, Jenny threw a hard long shot. It paid off for Serena.

"That's what I'm talking about," he said, praising her up. "You just need to slip that punch faster and focus on your center line."

The two fighters continued to spar with Pete throwing out encouraging words and a few interested boxers watching. Whilst all eyes were on the two sparer's, Holly and Topher had walked in and were studying Serena's moves.

"I bet my Holly could kick that ass," Topher shouted for everyone to hear.

Pete stopped the fighters from sparring and told Jenny that she had done a good job and that she could go. He then told Serena to take a two minute session on the heavy bag before her cool down. Serena removed her mouth guard and avoided saying anything to Topher or Holly, she knew it would just add to the fire. As she walked over to the heavy bag, she glared at Holly whilst Topher talked with Pete.

Holly was intimidated by Serena's stare, she'd seen that look when Serena was in the ring and it meant only one thing—Hatred!

"That's right, just walk away," Serena muttered to herself as she threw a jab into the bag. She did her two minute session and then finished off with her cool down exercises. Walking to the locker room, she caught sight of Holly staring at her again. She was starting to get pissed off with it so she acted in a childish manner and poked her tongue out at her. Holly, embarrassed, looked away.

"And who might you be poking your tongue at?" a female voice said behind her.

Serena turned around to find Ruth in front of her. "Oh you saw that? Now I look like an idiot."

"A cute one, if I may say so. I like your outfit."

"Do I detect a little flirtation going on here?" Serena asked.

"Maybe." Ruth swayed her hips angelically. "I do write lesbian erotica."

"Perhaps I should read some of your books."

"Perhaps you should."

"Okay, wait here. I have to take a shower and change. I'll be about fifteen minutes so why don't you go and check the gym out and I'll be out shortly."

Whilst Serena took a shower, Ruth took the opportunity to explore the gym. She watched a boxer punching a speed bag. He was muscular and fast with his oval punches. She then moved on to watch a sparring match and whilst she was fascinated with their training, she hadn't noticed that Holly had made her way behind her.

Although Holly was the one to have left Serena for what she had thought would be a better life, she still secretly had feelings toward her. Standing behind Ruth, she inhaled her perfume. Jealousy engulfed her as she knew that she was witnessing some sort of bond between her ex-girlfriend and this newcomer. She was beginning to feel regret for what she had done to Serena.

Ruth sensing that someone was standing behind her, turned and smiled at Holly.

"It draws you in, doesn't it?" Holly said to her.

"I'm sorry, what does?" Ruth replied, confused to what it was she supposed to be drawn to.

"Boxing, training, exercise, rhythm," Holly replied as she leaned in closer.

As Ruth was about to get further into conversation, Serena joined them. "Let's go, Ruth, I hope you weren't bored to death." She took Ruth by her arm and encouraged her to walk away.

"Bye," Ruth said innocently.

Holly attempted to talk to Serena but Serena chose to ignore her presence, so instead, she waved her hand and half-smiled. Serena quickly glanced back over her shoulder to look at Holly, then turned back to concentrate on her conversation with Ruth.

"Holly!" Topher shouted from the other side of the ring.

Holly snapped out of her gaze and immediately went over to him.

"Just what the hell was that about?" he barked at her.

"Nothing, I was just trying to be nice—."

"Nice doesn't cut it with me. Stay away from her, do you understand?"

"Hey, now wait a minute," Pete butted in. "You can't talk to her like that."

Topher's stance was intimidating with his arms crossed over his chest and his muscles pumped to their fullest. "I'll talk to her exactly how I want to. I'm her manager and her boyfriend. She knows what's good for her."

"Not in my gym, Topher. Just remember where you are." Pete shook his head disapprovingly at Holly, then headed off to his office.

"Yeah, well when are you going to set up a fight between Holly and that big headed tart?"

Pete ignored him.

Out in the car park Serena explained to Ruth the history between her and Holly and that she was finding it hard to refrain from saying anything to her about their sudden split. It was hard for Serena to watch Holly with her new found love interest because deep down, she was still in love with her.

"Whoa, you mean she passed on you to be with that big beast. That's kind of a low blow," Ruth said, angered by the mere fact that a lesbian would even think to go with a man, let alone one who looked like him. Serena's back was to the gym but Ruth was facing it and she saw Holly watching them through the window. "Quick, kiss me."

"What?" Serena quickly responded.

"Just do it now." She took hold of Serena by her jacket and pulled her toward her, then placing her hands around Serena's neck, she planted a kiss on her lips. She released her slowly. "There, that'll give her something to think about."

Serena went to look behind her to see who Ruth was talking about but Ruth stopped her and told her that Holly was watching them. Serena smiled. It felt good, even if it meant nothing, to give Holly something to be jealous of.

They decided to drive in separate cars to a coffee shop down the street. Serena drove ahead of Ruth to show her the way. Once inside, they sat at a table to the far back and chatted about things that they had in common. Serena discovered that Ruth liked some of the same TV shows that she did, which was already a plus over Holly, who hated most of the shows. Then Ruth discovered that Serena had an ex-girlfriend from way back who she herself had dated in recent years. They compared notes on their relationships with her. The conversation was light and pleasant and both women were truly enjoying themselves. The serene atmosphere was unexpectedly interrupted when Topher walked in and stood in the lineup to order himself a coffee. He looked over at the pair enjoying themselves and just couldn't resist bashing them publicly.

He walked over to their table as if he owned the place. "So I see you two are getting cozy. Well it's good to see that you're moving on from Holly who by the way can see you two from the car. Why don't you give her a nice wave, Serena?" he said menacingly.

"What is your problem?" Serena sneered.

"Name the date."

"Date for what?" Ruth asked.

"I won't fight her, now get out of my face."

"What's the matter, Serena, scared that she's better than you and can and will take your title?" he mocked.

"No fucking way will I ever be scared of Holly. She's not in my league and she knows it, why can't you see that and why are you pushing for her to fight me?"

"Because I can't stand you. Because I can't stand the fact that she went through a lesbian phase and it happened to be with you. What did you do to seduce her, I'm just curious how you turned a straight girl and believe me she is definitely straight in the bedroom department, into having sex with you."

"She didn't go through a phase, now if you don't mind, we're having a private conversation."

"Oh don't let her talk you into bed, little darlin', you don't fall for her mesmerising ways, you hear me now?" he said looking directly at Ruth.

"Well you had better hear this. I am a lesbian, I always have been and I always will be and for your information, Serena knows how to treat a woman in bed. God she fucked my brains out not more than an hour before she went to train today. I'm so fucking horny for her, hey babe, you made me come six times this morning, I'm hungry for some more of that hot loving you got down there."

"Sick bitch. The pair of you are disgusting. You need to seek psychiatric help." He backed away from their table, ordered his coffee and left the coffee shop.

Serena watched through the window as he reversed the car out of the space. Holly was staring at her and she didn't portray a picture of someone blissfully happy.

"I'm sorry, Serena, I just couldn't resist throwing that one in his face."

"They're not going to leave me alone, are they?" Serena whispered to herself.

Ruth heard what she said but couldn't offer her an answer. Serena stared at her phone that was in front of her on the table. She drummed her fingers next to it, then picked it up. She keyed Ricky's number and when he answered, she said, "Set it up. I'll fight her, jut set it up." Then she ended the call.

"But I thought that you just said you weren't going to fight her?" Ruth said, confused by Serena's decision.

Serena, with her elbows on the table, rested her head in her hands and leaned in close to Ruth. She looked directly into her eyes. "I want to fuck you."

Ruth's eyes widened and her cheeks blushed from embarrassment.

•••

The front door swung open at Serena's house and she and Ruth entered the hallway with their hands grabbing at each other's clothing, tugging and removing their shirts and casting them to the ground. Their lips were interlocked causing them both to breathe heavy. Serena led the way to the lounge, and still kissing, she backed Ruth onto the couch. Ruth fell backwards down onto the cushions and hurriedly unzipped her black skirt. Serena pulled it down her legs and threw it onto the armchair. Ruth was gorgeous in Serena's eyes and she wanted to kiss her from head to toe. She straddled over Ruth's legs and leaned in to kiss her hard, even tugging on her lip with her teeth. She slipped Ruth's bra straps from her shoulders and pulled the cups from her breasts, then continued to kiss her nipples and further herself down Ruth's body, over her stomach and to her panties. She pulled them down over Ruth's thighs and slipped them down her legs until they reached her ankles, leaving Ruth to kick them off. She parted her thighs and kissed further down, reaching the spot that Ruth was now craving to be touched.

Ruth grabbed Serena's hair and arching her back she cried out, "Oh god, fuck me!"

•••

It was late afternoon and Serena and Ruth had both fallen asleep, spooning and naked on the couch.

Seeing that the front door was wide open, Dawn walked straight in to be confronted by clothing strewn in the hallway and then shocked when she was presented with her sister and her lover showing off their naked assets.

"Serena!" she squealed.

Serena and Ruth both jolted from their sleep. Serena jumped off the couch and grabbed her jeans and speedily put them on, then searched around for her top.

"It's in the hallway," Dawn said covering her eyes with her one hand and pointing toward the hallway with the other.

Ruth grabbed a pillow that had been thrown on the floor and covered her lower region with it whilst Serena picked up her clothing and handed to her. She self-consciously threw her blouse over her shoulders and shoved her arms into the sleeves and then slipped her skirt up her legs and zipped it up. She got up from the couch and began to search for her panties.

"Are these what you're looking for?" Dawn asked, pointing at the fireplace where Ruth's panties and bra had been thrown to.

"Yes, thank you," she said softly. She picked them up and not wanting to embarrass herself any further, she sought her purse and shoved them inside. "Well that's the fastest that I've ever dressed."

'WOW! Does that mean you make a habit of doing this?" Dawn asked her.

Ruth, unsure on how to take that comment, immediately shook her head.

"Maybe next time you'll close the front door. Jesus, I could have been anyone walking in on you." She took out a tissue from her purse and wiped down the cushion in the armchair.

"I don't know what you think we did on that chair, Dawn," Serena told her sternly.

"Well I don't know what two women do together when, well when you know."

"No, I don't know, Dawn." Serena said.

"I beg to differ," Ruth said. "Hi, I'm Ruth, you must be Serena's sister." She held out her hand to shake.

Dawn shook her hand and then sat down in the chair, crossing her legs and resting her hands on top of her thighs. "So are you just a one night stand or is there something more serious to this?"

"Dawn, we fucked. There's been no discussion about anything else so can you please leave it."

Serena left the room and went into the kitchen. She filled the kettle with water and put it on. Whilst waiting for it to boil, she ground some coffee beans, then stared out of the window to see Rhonda once again walking her little dog. "Jesus, I had better not turn out to be as boring as her when I'm older."

Sprott had been asleep on Serena's bed and when he heard her enter the kitchen, he ran down the stairs and joined her. Making his usual figure eight ritual around her legs, he meowed for his breakfast. Serena opened a can and emptied it into his bowl.

The kettle boiled and she poured the fresh ground coffee into the pot and then poured the water over it.

"That coffee smells good from in here," Dawn shouted to her from the lounge.

Serena carried the three mugs and a bowl of sugar on a tray and placed it down on the coffee table. "I don't know if you take sugar or not," she said to Ruth.

"Oh I take it without but thank you."

Serena sat next to Ruth on the couch and there was a sense of awkwardness in the lack of conversation.

"Stick thin Cynthia gave Phil his marching orders and the cheeky bastard only tried to worm his way back into my life." Dawn informed them.

Serena picked up her coffee. "I hope you told him where to stick it."

"Yep. Sure did."

"I saw Holly today. She doesn't look happy."

"And her boyfriend challenged Serena to fight her and she has accepted it," Ruth informed her.

Dawn spat her coffee out, spraying it over her skirt. "You and Holly? What on earth made you change your mind?"

"I'm sick of that beef head that she left me for, constantly hounding me about it. I've had enough so I told Ricky to set it up."

"Speaking of Ricky," Dawn said, placing her mug back down onto the tray. "I've seen him a couple of times now. I can officially say that we are an item." She slapped her hands over her mouth, excited that she had some good news to tell her sister.

With that news being announced, Ricky texted Serena back with a date set for the fight. October 20th, four weeks from now.

CHAPTER SEVEN

Serena had been in intense training for the fight. Ruth had been her running partner, Pete had been giving her rigorous workouts and Ricky had been promoting the fight through all social media outlets and local radio stations and newspapers.

Serena was at a local radio station being interviewed live on air.

"You're listening to RanTrax Radio and I'm Chrystal Mayers and today's special guest is Serena Ward, who, if you haven't already heard of her, where the hell have you been, folks? She is the champion in her sports, and that would be boxing. Welcome Serena." Chrystal signalled for her to speak by counting down her fingers from three to one.

Serena, seated on the other side of the desk, leaned forward to her microphone. "Hello, Chrystal, and hello to all of your listeners, and my fans if any of you are listening today."

"Oh, I'm sure there's plenty, Serena. WOW I can honestly say folks, she's a hottie. It's official, you heard it here first."

"Oh, Chrystal please stop, you're making me blush."

"So, Serena, what's it like to be in that ring and your adrenaline is pumped to its fullest and then you get punched in the face? I mean really, do you feel the pain immediately or is there some sort of delay?"

"Good question. Well yes of course adrenaline plays a big role in how you respond to being hit. I think my face must be made of stone or something as I rarely feel the pain at the time, it's usually later, when I get home sometimes, that's when everything sinks in."

"So how do you feel about your upcoming fight against Pink Leopard, or more commonly known as Holly Blackwell, she's your ex-girlfriend, isn't she?"

"Yes she is. I don't feel any different than I would toward another fighter to be honest. I have a job to do and so does she. It'll be interesting to say the least."

"I'm one of those people who have a passion for a happy ending, do you think that the two of you will reconcile after this fight?"

"I think what we had, came to a natural end. It just wasn't meant to be. I just hope that she's happy now and got what she was looking for."

"Aww, bless, that's so sweet of you to think of her like that. Now her trainer, Topher Emerson has been reported to be a bit of a trouble maker between the two of you. Do you think that this will affect yours or her performance?"

"As I said, Chrystal, I'm treating her as any other fighter. How she's dealing with this, well I guess you should ask her."

"Pink Leopard, if you're listening now, please call the station. It would be great to have the two of you talk live on air."

"I don't think—."

"Oh, wait! My producer is signalling to me that Pink Leopard is on the phone right now. Pink Leopard, or should I call you Holly, how are you?"

'Hi, Chrystal. I'm good, how are you?'

"Never mind how I am, nobody wants to hear about me. So tell me, Holly, how do you think this fight is going to go?"

'I'll tell you after I win, Chrystal.'

"Oh, so you think you're going to take the title from Serena?"

'Most definitely. It's time for her to move over and let the hungrier fighters take the lead. Hi, Serena.'

Serena glared at Chrystal. She paused and then removed her sweater. "Hi, Holly."

'It's good to hear your voice but I can tell you now, you're going down.' Holly bragged.

"Whatever, Holly, just dream on, girl, just dream on."

'Oh I'm dreaming about what I'm going to take from you, Serena. I can almost smell it.'

"Well, you heard it here, folks, these two ladies are raring to fight it out in the ring. If you haven't already, then go and buy your tickets and support these two women. Thank you for sharing with us, Serena and Holly, and keep it a clean fight."

"Thank you, Chrystal," Serena said, getting up from her seat. She shook her hand and left the room feeling slightly deflated from having to listen to Holly attempting to brag that she was going to win. Even though it was expected from both sides, Serena didn't want to have to talk to her directly.

Walking down the hallway, she was stopped by Chrystal calling after her from the doorway.

"Hey, Serena."

Serena turned. "Yes?"

"I just wanted to say, off the record, my money's on you." She smiled and disappeared back into the room.

Serena smiled to herself and feeling a twinge of self-satisfaction, she carried on walking to the elevator. When she got into her car, she turned the radio on and changed it to RanTrax Radio station. Chrystal was still talking about the interview that she had just held live between Serena and Holly and how surprised she was to be in the presence of such a graceful woman as she had expected Serena to have appeared more masculine than she actually was. She then went on to state that she was pleasantly amazed with her guest. Serena drove home feeling extremely contented.

When she arrived home, she was greeted by Ruth who was sat on her front doorstep. Ruth was in her running gear, ready for their arranged session. Serena got out of her car and apologized for keeping her waiting. She hurried inside her house, ran up to her bedroom, changed, grabbed a bottle of water and then the two were headed for the local parkland on foot.

They ran down the hill and then into the wooded area and along the dirt track.

"I heard your interview today," Ruth said.

"Yeah, what did you think?"

"She was flirting with you, I could tell."

Serena laughed. "Do I detect a little jealousy?"

"Perhaps," Ruth replied with a smile.

They ran beneath a line of trees, it was the same area where Serena had first met Ruth. Serena came to a halt and took a drink of water, Ruth remained running on the spot to keep her muscles warm.

"I don't think it's right for you to be waiting on my doorstep for me," Serena told her.

"But what should I do?"

"I'm going to give you a key to let yourself in. I think I can trust you enough."

"Really? You mean as in taking it to the next level kind of thing?"

"Yes, you've grown on me." Serena laughed.

"Oh my god, Serena, I love you."

Serena was surprised to hear those words arise in the conversation. Ruth had caught her off guard, she wasn't ready for it to be that serious just yet. "Come on, let's continue our run."

•••

Serena was in full training mode working out at Pete's gym. Her biceps were pumped from using the bench press, her stomach taught from crunches, and her calf's strengthened from leg raises. Her stamina and strength were at an all-time high after punching into the heavy bag and her eye and hand co-ordination were perfect when she rolled her punches into the speed bag.

Pete tapped her on her shoulder. "I think you're ready, Serena."

•••

Serena, Ricky and Pete were in the locker room and could hear the fans cheering for the fight to start. Ricky was on his phone answering to social media questions and posting messages of his own that Viper Girl was in fighting fit condition and excited to be up against Pink Leopard. There were messages from Topher, stating that Viper Girl was history and was no competition for Pink Leopard. Ricky laughed at his allusions.

It was time for their weigh-in. Pink Leopard went first and stood on the scale. She weighed 134lbs then Viper Girl stood on the scale and weighed-in at 135lbs. Pink Leopard tried to maintain an aggressive behavior, egged on by Topher. But her taunting words were falling on deaf ears as far as Viper Girl was concerned. She remained calm and collective, listening only to her inner thoughts and the encouraging words from Ricky and Pete.

Their gloves were on and approved by the commission.

Viper Girl sat on her stool in her corner of the ring. Ricky and Pete were knelt either side of her, giving her all the advice they had. She stared at Pink Leopard, psyching her out and she was sure that there was a moment that she may have shown a glimmer of fear in eyes, but Topher was quick to change that with his apparent pep talk with her.

Dawn, her mother and Ruth were seated in the front row, cheering Viper Girl on. Ruth wasn't sure if she should be excited that she was there to watch her girlfriend fight live, or if she should be concerned that Serena may need medical attention after this.

The stadium was filled and many fans were holding their cameras up, recording what they could and sending the footage out to their social networks. Reporters were down at the ringside and the judges were seated, ready for the fight to begin.

Two scantily clad women walked around the ring holding 'Round 1' placards above their heads, both of them flirting with the crowd and the cameras. The ring announcer introduced both fighters, declaring their weight, height, nicknames and their win/loss records.

The ref signalled for the fight to start and Pete shoved the mouth guard into Viper Girls mouth. Whistling and cheering came from the crowd as both girls got up from their stools and stepped forward. With the fight officially underway, the girls circled, both were very aware of each other's talents.

Pink Leopard's fighting style was different from Viper Girl's. She was known as a counter puncher, a slippery style of fighter who rely on their opponent to make a mistake so they can gain an advantage. She had a well-rounded defense and used it to avoid or block shots, then catch her opponent off guard with a well-timed punch.

Viper Girl threw the first jab, Pink Leopard was able to block it, they circled, then Viper Girl tilted back, Pink Leopard threw a long shot and Viper Girl cut in a jab, landing a hard shot to Pink Leopard's cheek. Viper Girl lead in with a jab and quickly proceeded to grab Pink Leopard, the ref shouted, 'Break.' They circled, then Viper Girl moved her left foot forward and sent a straight powerful shot with her left hand, directly hitting Pink Leopard on her nose. Not giving her any time to react, she sent in a second powerful straight, placing her punch to the eye. Pink Leopard swayed backwards. The ref signalled the end of round one.

Both fighters sat on their stools. The cut doctor tended to Pink Leopard's eye. Pete and Ricky praised Viper Girl for her attacking qualities.

The two ring girls paced around the ring holding 'Round 2' placards.

Round two began. The fighters stepped up and circled. Pink Leopards eye was swollen and it was hard for her to see out of it. Viper Girl gave the impression that she was sending in a straight but instead fooled her opponent by using her lead hand and landed a powerful blow. Pink Leopard's head snapped back when she received the sharp shot to her eye. It caused her brow to split.

Because Pink Leopard was in a weakened state, Viper Girl seized the opportunity and putting all of her weight behind it, she cocked the back of her hand for extra extension and delivered a wide semi-circular punch with great force. Pink Leopard was unable to counter the move.

Pink Leopard was unsteady on her feet, she tried to lunge in but Viper Girl pivoted on her left foot and turned and hooked at the same time. As Pink Leopard moved in, Viper Girl landed a shot. The force was powerful as it hit the eye area once again. Pink Leopard was fast on the floor.

The ref counted to ten. Pink Leopard was out cold. Viper Girls arms were raised in the air by the ref and declared the winner of the fight. Her eyes immediately looked at Topher who was crouched at Pink Leopards side, trying to bring her to.

The ring announcer climbed in and announced that the winner was still the champion.

Ricky and Pete jumped into the ring, both screaming and shouting and threw their arms around Viper Girl, hugging her hard. Pete held one of his hands out for Viper Girl to spit her mouth guard into.

Pink Leopard opened her eyes and Topher helped her to her feet. He and the cut doctor carried her to her stool and sat her down. She was dazed and confused.

Concerned about Holly's welfare, Serena tried to peer over Ricky's shoulder. "Is she okay?"

Ricky looked over his shoulder to see Holly leaving the ring with Topher. He turned back to Serena and nodded with a smile. "I think her pride might have taken a beating though."

Dawn, her mother and Ruth, screamed and cheered with the crowd as the three of them hurried to the edge of the ring to congratulate Serena, all three of them were excitedly talking to her at the same time. Serena couldn't understand what they were saying and found it amusing.

Dawn reached for her ankle through the ropes to get her attention. "You showed her, Serena, you really got your payback, good for you."

•••

Three days had passed. It was late afternoon and Serena and Ruth were relaxed on the lounger and enjoying the sun, when Serena's phone buzzed. She picked it up and saw that the caller was Holly.

"Shit! What does she want?"

"Who?" Ruth asked, sitting up and peering over the top of her sunglasses.

"It's Holly." Serena waited a moment and then answered the call. "Hello?"

'Hi, Serena. I really wasn't sure if you were going to answer my call or not.'

"Well I did. Why are you calling me?"

'I wanted to let you know that it wasn't me who pressed for the fight. Topher, well he's jealous that we had a relationship——.'

"I don't give a shit about Topher's behavioral problems. What are you calling for?"

'I just wanted to say that I'm sorry. I'm sorry for everything that I put you through, it wasn't fair of me to leave you the way that I did and then for Topher to flaunt it in your face. I truly did love you, I hope you can believe that.'

"I've moved on, Holly. I'm with someone else now. Yeah I will admit that you hurt me. We went through a lot together and I thought that we were happy, well I was anyway. But now—I really couldn't give a crap about you."

'Oh? Well I'm glad you're happy now.'

"Yes I am. Is there anything else that you want, Holly?"

'No. I'll just wish you a happy life and I hope everything works out between you and your new girlfriend, she seems really nice.'

"Bye, Holly." Serena put her phone down next to her drink on the table.

"So I take it that you've found closure with her?" Ruth asked.

"I like you a lot, Ruth, and perhaps in the near future I will be able to let my walls down with you. She hurt me and—."

"I understand," Ruth replied serenely.

Serena lay back down in the lounger and smiled at Ruth. She knew that by finally closing the door on Holly, she would now be able to concentrate on her own future and building her relationship with Ruth—one day at a time.

The End

ABOUT THE AUTHOR

I love to write and when I have an underlying passion for certain subjects, I find that no matter what, it just has to be penned. I now have a numerous amount of books written in the lesbian genre, ranging from simple Victorian romances, through-to erotic, contemporary and also hard-core BDSM.

Thank you for reading my story and if you enjoyed it please feel free to leave a review on the site that you purchased it from.

Have you read Pink Crush? Download a sample and connect with Danny Cooper, a female fire-fighter.

The Dark Cully's Mistress. A Victorian romance with love, murder and plot twists you won't see coming.

I also have several lesbian erotic/BDSM short stories published. Check them out on your favourite site, just type in my author name to view my collection.

I began to write, because as a lesbian, there really isn't that much to watch on TV that suites my enjoyment. Loving the Pink Kiss was my first published book and differs from any other that I have in my collection, due to the pure fact that I used my life story and wanted to share it with you. I have written several short erotic/BDSM stories and concentrate on ideas and situations that I find myself fantasising about. Pink Crush was my second novel and all though I began to write it immediately after finishing Loving the Pink Kiss, you will see this is where the trend begins towards my darker side.

As I finish one book, I find that I have already got ideas swimming around in my head for the next. And what I tend to do, is play the storyline out in my head for a few days as if I was watching a live play, with me being the producer and changing the scenes if I'm not happy with them.

Shiralyn J. Lee

Published Books

The Dark Cully's Mistress

Pink Crush

Pink Seduction

The Submissive Scullery Maid

Vampire Changeling

Erotic Spirits

She's on the Ball

Ruby Tipped Globes

A Victorian Romance

The Dark Cully's Mistress

Paige Bleu Series, Case 321, Case 503, Case 16, Case 537

Sex, Ropes and Chains, Book 1, Book 2, Book 3, Book 4.

Stop! In The Name Of Love

Tell Me What To Do

Touching Gloves

Lesbian in Question

Touching Gloves
Shiralyn J. Lee

Touching Gloves
Shiralyn J. Lee

Printed in Great Britain
by Amazon.co.uk, Ltd.,
Marston Gate.